Dolphin Diaries™

Ben M. Baglio

Illustrations by Judith Lawton

LEAVING
THE SHALLOWS

AN
APPLE
PAPERBACK

SCHOLASTIC INC.
New York Toronto London Auckland Sydney
Mexico City New Delhi Hong Kong Buenos Aires

Special thanks to Lucy Courtenay

No part of this publication may be reproduced in whole or in part, or stored in a retrieval system, or transmitted in any form or by any means, electronic, mechanical, photocopying, recording, or otherwise, without written permission of the publisher. For information regarding permission, write to Working Partners Limited, 1 Albion Place, London W6 0QT, United Kingdom.

ISBN 0-439-44616-3

12 11 10 9 8 7 6 5 4 3   3 4 5 6 7 8/0

Printed in the U.S.A.   40
First Scholastic printing, January 2003

1

March 12 — morning — Pacific Ocean (still)
Everyone got a surprise this morning. Out of nowhere, a flying fish landed on the deck with a huge flopping noise and started thrashing around. It was enormous, with beautiful silvery wings. Everyone yelled and ran around until Cam managed to scoop it up and throw it back into the sea. I wonder, what it was running away from? Something very hungry, I bet!

Jody McGrath closed her diary thoughtfully and played with the little silver dolphin she always wore around her neck. The flying fish had been magnificent. The ocean had a habit of throwing surprises at you like that. There was a real mystery about the deep blue water, which Jody knew she'd never fully understand.

Dolphin Dreamer had left the Marquesas Islands in Polynesia four weeks ago. Even after four weeks at sea, the waves still fascinated Jody. Calm one day and wild the next. Sometimes lit by sunsets and sometimes by moonlight. Jody thought she'd never get bored of looking at them.

She put away her diary and climbed up into the open air. The deck was warm under her feet and the sun was bright, though the glare from the sea hurt her eyes after the cool of her cabin. She blinked, adjusting to the light. "Anyone out here?" she asked.

"Yes — and trying to get some peace and quiet, *actually,*" came a sarcastic voice.

Jody looked up and saw Brittany Pierce sunbathing on the cabin roof. Brittany was thirteen and very spoiled. Jody tried hard to like her, but it was difficult. She was so moody! Still, you couldn't really blame her, Jody thought. Her mother had gone to Paris without any warning and had dumped Brittany on her father, Harry, the captain of *Dolphin Dreamer.* That had been nine months ago. Brittany had been much better recently, but the long weeks at sea were beginning to get on her nerves.

"Have you seen Sean and Jimmy?" Jody asked. Her twin brothers had been making trouble for more than a week. At eight years old, they were not very good at dealing with boredom.

Brittany groaned. "Don't ask. They have been whispering together for the past half hour about something or other." She rolled her eyes. "I mean, they are *so* immature!" She turned over onto her front with a sigh.

Jody looked around the deck. Cameron Tucker, the first mate, was mending a sail. Harry Pierce was examining a chart.

"Where are we, Harry?" Jody asked, looking over his shoulder.

Harry smiled at her. "Miles from anywhere," he said cheerfully. "But we're making good time, given the distances we've been covering."

"When will all this sea stop?" Brittany complained. "I'm sick of staring at waves all day long."

3

Harry pointed straight ahead. "Well, you'll be pleased to know that we're almost at the east coast of Australia."

Australia! Jody thought of all the wonderful marine life that Australia was famous for. Dolphins, sharks, rays — and wonderful coral reefs, too.

"Is that where we're going next?" she asked.

Harry looked surprised. "Haven't your parents told you?"

"I know we're going to Australia," said Jody. "I just don't know which part." She frowned. "It seems like Mom and Dad haven't decided yet."

Harry's eyes twinkled. "I don't blame them. Australia is such a diverse place, especially for marine biologists." He sighed. "Choices, choices!"

Jody stared at him. "But *you* know where we're going, don't you?" she asked suddenly.

"Me?" Harry pretended to look confused. "I'm just the skipper. I'm quite happy sailing around in circles."

Jody laughed. "Very funny!" she joked. "You know, don't you? Of course you do! Come on, tell me!"

"Go on, Dad," Brittany added from the cabin roof. "I need to hear something to cheer me up."

Harry put his hand on his heart. "I promised your mom and dad that I wouldn't breathe a word. You'd better go and ask them yourselves," he said to Jody.

Jody's heart gave a little skip of excitement. She loved surprises. Just what exactly were her parents planning?

Suddenly, she heard Sean's voice. "Hey, Jimmy!"

Sean was standing innocently on the deck. There was something about his expression that immediately made Jody suspicious.

Jimmy popped up from behind one of the masts. "Yes, Sean?"

"Have you seen that very big bug lately?" Sean inquired.

Jody frowned. A bug? From her vantage point next to Harry, she could see Brittany's back stiffen at the mention of bugs. She hated bugs, as Jimmy and Sean knew.

Jimmy looked interested. "You mean that very huge bug we've been talking about?"

Sean nodded vigorously. "I think it's a spider, actually," he confided. "It had lots of legs last time I saw it."

Brittany's back got stiffer.

"It must be very hungry," observed Jimmy casually. "After all, we haven't seen land for four weeks. It's probably eaten all the other bugs on board already. I bet it'll be looking for food."

Jody began to feel worried. A spider? She knew Polynesia had some big spiders. Could one have gotten on board without anyone noticing?

"Well," Sean continued, "we'd better keep an eye out for it. In case it's dangerous, you know," he concluded.

Jimmy nodded. "Definitely," he said.

Suddenly, Sean's eyes grew round. "There!" he shouted, pointing across the deck. A sprawling, leggy, black shape was lying in the shadow of the main mast.

"Aaaaah!" Brittany shrieked, leaping to her feet. "A spider! Get it away from me!"

Jody looked closer. The spider didn't seem to be moving. It was lying ominously still. In fact, now that she could see it more clearly . . .

"It's netting!" she exclaimed. "Just a piece of old black netting!"

Britt gets a nasty surprise

Jimmy and Sean exploded with laughter. "Got you!" they cried gleefully, before giving each other high fives.

Brittany looked upset. "I-I-I think you're awful!" she cried, bursting into tears. "I hate you!" With that, she fled belowdecks, sobbing noisily.

"Boys!" Jody said crossly, trying not to smile. "You know Brittany's scared of spiders. That was really mean."

"But it wasn't a real spider," Jimmy said bluntly. "It was just pretend."

"Yes, but Brittany didn't know that," Jody began.

But Jimmy and Sean were already sidling off. They had spotted Dr. Jefferson Taylor snoozing at the far end of the deck. His round red face was covered by his hat, and Jody could hear him gently snoring. Dr. Taylor was a scientist who had been sent on this research trip as a representative of PetroCo, *Dolphin Dreamer*'s sponsor.

Somehow, Jody didn't have the heart to stop Jimmy and Sean's fun. She hesitated as she went below, wondering whether to go and check on Brittany or find her parents so she could ask them where *Dolphin Dreamer* was heading. It was a tough decision.

With a sigh, she turned and knocked on the door of the cabin she shared with Brittany. There was no answer. She knocked again, more loudly this time.

"Go away!" Brittany's voice sounded thick and miserable.

Jody opened the cabin door a fraction. A pillow whistled through the air and crashed into the door, making her jump.

"I said, GO AWAY!" Brittany repeated stubbornly. "I don't want to talk to you."

"Jimmy and Sean are just bored," Jody pointed out. "They didn't mean any harm. Are you OK?"

Brittany's face crumpled. "N-n-no!" she cried, covering her face with her one remaining pillow. "I want my mom. I hate this stupid ship, and I wish I'd never come!" she finished, turning her face to the cabin wall.

Jody decided to leave Brittany alone for a while and quietly closed the cabin door. She'd have a word with Sean and Jimmy later and make them apologize. Brittany hated being teased and would be grumpy for the rest of the trip unless Jody tried to make peace.

She wandered down to the office, where she found her mother hunched over the ship's computer. Gina McGrath was often found updating their web site, Dolphin Universe, with the latest news on their research trip.

"Come on, Mom," Jody said immediately. "The game's up. You know where we're going. Harry said so!" She sat next to her mother. "Why the big secret?"

Gina grinned. "How do you know we're going anywhere?" she asked. "There's plenty of work we could do out here in the ocean, you know."

Jody opened her mouth to protest, but Gina put a finger to her lips and pointed at the computer screen. It wasn't showing the familiar home page of Dolphin Universe. Instead, Jody was staring at a photograph of a place she'd never seen before.

Long white sandy beaches stretched away from a beautiful blue sea. Palm trees waved against a deep blue sky. The color of the water varied from pale turquoise to a deep indigo as the seabed sloped away. With a leap of excitement, Jody realized that this must be their secret destination.

"Come on, Mom," she begged. "Where is it? Stop keeping us in suspense!"

Gina scrolled farther down the page, coming to a stop on an image of an enormous creature leaping out of the waves with a crash. "Hervey Bay, Queensland. And this is what Hervey Bay is really famous for," she said.

"It's a whale!" Jody exclaimed, leaning in closer.

"Hervey Bay is one of the most famous places in the world for whale watching," said Gina. "Humpback whales migrate to the warm waters of the bay to escape the harsh Antarctic winter."

"Wonderful!" Jody exclaimed. The humpback whale in the picture was *enormous.* She couldn't believe how powerful it must be to leap out of the sea like that. "Will we see any?"

Gina shook her head regretfully. "Unfortunately, we're too early — or too late, depending on how you look at it. They come to breed between August and October. But Hervey Bay is much more than just a whale-watching site."

She clicked on another picture, and Jody grinned to see a family of dolphins swimming through the pale, clear water.

"The sea around Hervey Bay is a marine nature reserve," Gina explained. "There are dolphins, orcas, rays, dugongs, and sharks, among other things."

Jody stared at the picture. "So if it's a nature reserve, are they wild dolphins?"

"Yup." Gina clicked on another image, which showed a female dolphin swimming beside her calf. "It's amazing, isn't it? And perfect for a vacation!"

11

A vacation! So *that* was the big surprise!

"You mean, a vacation for us?" Jody asked excitedly.

"Of course." Gina swung around from the computer screen and took Jody's hands. "Your dad booked a mooring for *Dolphin Dreamer* last night, in the harbor of Oceans Point, one of Hervey Bay's best resorts. We didn't want to get your hopes up before we had finalized everything. Don't you think we deserve a break?"

Jody thought of the long weeks at sea. She thought about how hard her parents had been working since they had all set off on this research trip last summer, and how wonderful it would be to stay in one place for a little while.

But Jody had one small doubt in her mind. "No work at all?" she said. She looked at the computer screen again. "Not even with the Hervey Bay dolphins?"

Gina laughed. "Do you really think we'd be in Hervey Bay and not visit the dolphins? We couldn't ignore them if we tried! But it'll still be a vacation for everyone. Jimmy and Sean need to work off some steam, and Harry and the crew could use a break. I think you could, too. What do you think?"

Before Jody had a chance to reply, there was a bellow from the deck, and Dr. Taylor flew down the cabin steps at top speed.

Gina leaped to her feet in concern. "Dr. Taylor? Is everything all right?"

Dr. Taylor took several deep breaths to compose himself. "There's a spider on deck," he managed to gasp. "I've never seen anything so enormous. I mean," he amended, "I'm not afraid of spiders or anything, of course not. But this one is very large. I'm concerned for everyone else. . . ."

Jimmy's and Sean's laughter floated down into the cabin. Dr. Taylor's face colored to a deep red as he realized that he had been tricked.

Jody turned to her mother. "I think you're right," she said. "We really *could* use a break!"

2

March 15 — morning — just off the coast of Oceans Point, Hervey Bay, Queensland

We've sighted Oceans Point at last! Just as dawn was breaking this morning, a thin blue line appeared on the horizon. I can see why sailors in the old days used to think they were seeing clouds instead of land — it didn't look real, somehow. Everyone's been talking about Hervey Bay since Mom and Dad broke the news. It sounds like the most incredible place. It's more of a marine reserve than a tourist resort, with lots of important ecological projects going on. Dr. Taylor doesn't think we should *be taking a vacation "at PetroCo's expense," as he puts it. Dad was very firm with him, pointing out that we've made good time across the Pacific and we all need a break.*

Jody couldn't tear her eyes away from the coast as *Dolphin Dreamer* finally sailed into the Oceans Point harbor. Palm trees lined the shore, but in a natural, muddled sort of way that Jody immediately preferred to all the pictures of expensive, groomed holiday resorts she'd ever seen. Several faded clapboard buildings lined the small harbor, with signs dotted along the pavement advertising whale-watching trips. The sand on either side of the harbor was almost pure white, and where the water touched the beach, it was so transparent that Jody had to squint to tell where the land ended and the water began.

A shoal of brightly colored fish darted under the hull of *Dolphin Dreamer,* following one another's quick movements like a troupe of well-trained ballet dancers. The whole place reminded Jody a little of the Caribbean, where they'd spent some time at the beginning of the research trip. But everything here looked lusher somehow and rich with the promise of marine life that even the Caribbean would have found hard to beat.

Away to the left, Jody could see the coast of Fraser Island, stretching back out into the ocean. She'd read that Fraser Island was the world's largest natural island made entirely out of sand. Despite this, it somehow managed to sustain a lush green rain forest and several freshwater lakes. It looked as magical as it had sounded when she'd read about it on the Internet.

"Land at last!" Brittany sighed dramatically. She pulled her sunglasses down from her head and perched them on the end of her nose. "I need to see different faces before I explode." She looked across at Jody. "I guess all you're interested in are the fish," she said, shaking her head. "You've got so much to learn, kiddo."

Jody ignored her, watching as Harry gently steered *Dolphin Dreamer* into her berth. They would be here for a week, and she intended to enjoy every second. Not even Brittany could annoy her now.

"So this is it, is it?" said Dr. Taylor fussily. He adjusted his sun hat and peered at the coastline. "Not much going on."

16

Craig McGrath, Jody's father, stepped up on deck behind Dr. Taylor. "And isn't it wonderful?" he said.

With a gentle splutter, *Dolphin Dreamer*'s engine came to a stop. Harry and Cam leaped down onto the pontoon and quickly fastened the ropes. Suddenly, they were all enveloped in a lovely feeling of calm, with only the gentle sound of lapping water and clinking ropes disturbing the air.

Craig clapped his hands. "Now that we're here, who's ready for the beach?"

"Me! Me!" Sean and Jimmy hopped around the deck. They were slightly hindered by the flippers and goggles they'd put on first thing that morning, as soon as they'd sighted land.

"I've got some business with the harbormaster," said Harry. "Don't worry about me."

Mei Lin, the ship's cook and engineer, shaded her eyes to look at the shops along the harbor. "I need to stock up on a few provisions," she said. "After so long at sea, we are really low on everything. Among other things, we could use some fresh fruit — and fresh bread, too. I can get a great lunch together for the first time in weeks!"

17

Jody's mouth watered at the thought. It had been so long since she'd tasted fresh warm bread or a sweet juicy orange.

Dr. Taylor stood uncertainly on the deck. "I don't think I'll come to the beach," he said gravely. "But a gentle stroll and stretching my legs on the promenade would be nice." He looked at the clapboard shops and buildings that stretched colorfully along the harbor front. "Maybe I'll be able to pick up some flyers on marine projects to add to my PetroCo dossier."

"Good," said Mei Lin promptly. "Then you'll be able to help me carry back the food, won't you, Dr. Taylor?"

Jody stifled a laugh at Dr. Taylor's expression. It was clear that his idea of a relaxing walk along the harbor hadn't included carrying back the groceries!

Gina turned to Jody and Brittany. "Dr. Taylor's right about stretching our legs. It'll do us all good to be on land for a change."

"You bet it will," said Brittany immediately.

Jody needed no further invitation. She jumped nimbly down onto the pontoon. "Are you coming, Maddie?" she called over her shoulder.

Maddie was Craig and Gina's assistant and had been tutoring Jody, Brittany, and the boys so that they didn't fall behind on any schoolwork. "You try to stop me." She smiled, putting a dollop of sunscreen on her slender black legs.

After Cam decided to join the beach party as well, it was a large group that made its way up to the harbor front. Jody stared at the local people and tourists strolling past. There were lots of different faces, with ruddy tans and freckles. Brittany was right. Much as she loved everyone on board *Dolphin Dreamer,* it was great to see something different for a change.

When they reached the harbor front, Dr. Taylor turned to the rest of the group. "Here is where we part, I think," he said. "I'll make my way along the front here, and then head back to the boat. I have some work I should be catching up on."

Mei Lin raised an eyebrow at him.

"Not forgetting the groceries, of course," he added with a nervous laugh. "Enjoy yourselves."

"Oh, we will," Gina assured him. "We most certainly will!"

Jody grinned to herself. Dr. Taylor made enjoyment sound like a criminal offense. He was OK once you got to know him, but he always acted a little uptight.

Jody followed the others toward the beach, walking slowly along the harbor front. The feel of solid ground under her feet was wonderful, though part of her still felt as if she were rocking from side to side. Finding her land legs after four weeks at sea would be a challenge. She found that she had lots of energy, and she wanted to run and shout — just like Sean and Jimmy were doing.

"Why did those little rats have to come?" complained Brittany, talking about the twins as she followed Jody along the harbor front. "They'll make a lot of noise and probably throw sand around. We won't get a second's peace. It'll be like being on board the boat again."

"They are only eight," Gina reminded Brittany as they made their way down a set of rickety wooden steps onto the beach.

"I'm sure I wasn't nearly so much trouble when I was eight," Brittany muttered.

With a sigh of pleasure, Jody felt the warm, soft sand sliding over the edges of her flip-flops. She kicked them off and felt the warmth along the whole underside of her foot.

They found a spot under a shady palm tree, where they laid out their towels. Sean and Jimmy immediately tore into the sea with loud whoops.

"Urgh," said Brittany. She looked around. "I'm going to sunbathe on that rock over there," she said at last, indicating a smooth dry rock sticking out into the sea. "Away from the sand and away from the *kids.*"

Jody watched Brittany walk carefully along the beach and make her way out to the rock. She hadn't even taken off her flip-flops.

"Don't forget to use lots of sunscreen!" Gina called after her. "The sun gets so hot, you can't be too careful," she said worriedly. "Do you think she'll be all right?"

Maddie took off her sundress and straightened the straps of her bathing suit. "Don't worry, Gina," she said. "I'll go for a swim by the rock and keep an eye on her. It's only nine-thirty — the sun isn't too hot at the moment. Brittany is too sensible to burn."

And too vain, thought Jody with an inward grin.

"I'll join you, Maddie," Cam said.

The water looked inviting, particularly when the sun shone through the sparkling droplets that flew up as Cam dived in. Jody stared thoughtfully at the gleaming waves.

"Go on, then," said Gina, noticing her daughter's expression. "Go have a swim. Just stay where we can see you, OK?"

The sea was just as cool as Jody had hoped. She waded out into deeper water and dived down below the surface. Twisting and turning like a fish, she savored every second of it. When she surfaced at last and floated calmly on the top of the water, Jody decided that she'd never felt so relaxed in her whole life.

She heard a familiar clicking sound somewhere on her right. Immediately alert, she looked around expectantly. Dolphins! This was her lucky day. She hadn't expected to see them so soon.

About five yards farther out to sea, the water heaved, and Jody gasped with delight to see a waving flipper of a dolphin breach the surface of the water. With a powerful beat of its tail, the dolphin leaped into the air. After its somersault, it cut cleanly back into the water again.

Although it had a slender bottle-shaped beak, Jody knew immediately it wasn't a bottle-nosed dolphin — the coloring looked wrong. So what was it?

Jody paddled a little to one side so that she was facing in the right direction, in case the dolphin reappeared. She knew that you should never approach a wild dolphin, and she was careful to keep her distance.

Floating peacefully!

23

The dolphin emerged again and floated for a moment on the surface of the water, breathing gently through its blowhole. Jody was intrigued to see that it had an interesting outline, with a pronounced bump on its head and a strange, fatty hump just below its fin. It was an unusual color, too — splashed pink and white.

The dolphin dipped below the surface of the water again, and Jody watched the water ripple away in its wake. Intrigued, she paddled gently around the area on her back. Would it come back a third time?

"Hey!"

Startled, she turned around to see a figure swimming toward her. When he stopped to tread water, Jody saw from his dark green armband that he was one of the wardens she had noticed on the beach earlier. He had an anxious expression on his face, which made Jody's stomach turn over.

"Stay exactly where you are!" he shouted. "Don't move, OK?"

Jody froze. She knew the tone of his voice meant something serious. And the first thing she thought was — *sharks*!

3

"Can you move away from the dolphin, please?" the warden asked, when he finally reached Jody.

"Where's the shark?" Jody said anxiously, looking all around her.

The warden looked surprised. "Shark?" he said. "There's no shark. Just you and a dolphin. I need you to move away, please."

With a rush of relief, Jody realized what had happened. There was no shark! She started giggling — she couldn't help it.

"It's no laughing matter," said the warden sternly, a

perplexed frown crossing his tanned face. "Approaching wild dolphins can be really dangerous."

Jody laughed helplessly. "I'm sorry," she managed to
gasp. "I thought there was a shark. I thought you were
coming to rescue me!" Then, because of the shock, she
dissolved into laughter again.

At last, she gained control of herself. "I'm really
sorry," she said again. "It's just that I would never in a
million years approach a wild dolphin. I've grown up
with dolphins, you see. I know the rules."

Jody swam back to shore with the warden, who introduced himself as Brice. He worked at Oceans Point,
running tours and keeping an eye on things, along
with his boss, David.

"So what brings you here?" Brice asked when the
water became shallow enough to walk through.

Jody explained all about *Dolphin Dreamer,* her parents, and how she'd spent the past nine months traveling around the world and visiting research sites in the
Caribbean, South America, and Polynesia.

Brice clapped his hand to his forehead. "I've heard

about you guys!" he said. "My boss got an e-mail from your dad, now that I think about it."

"Dad can't resist contacting fellow dolphin fans, even when we're on vacation!" Jody laughed as they waded back onto the beach. The sand felt doubly hot after the coolness of the water.

"So what do you think of Oceans Point and your vacation so far?" asked Brice, combing a hand through his tangled blond hair.

Jody thought about how calm she had felt as she watched the strange pink-and-white dolphin leaping out of the water. "Wonderful," she said honestly, looking back out to sea.

"That was Dawn you saw out there," Brice said. "Her Latin name is *Sousa chinensis,* although she's better known as the speckled or Indo-Pacific humpbacked dolphin."

"A humpbacked dolphin?" Jody remembered the strange bump on Dawn's back. "I didn't know there were humpbacked dolphins as well as humpback whales. Are they rare?"

"We don't know exactly how many humpbacks are out there," said Brice, "but we do know that they are divided into two types. In the western Pacific, they usually have a hump. In the east, they don't, but they have a taller fin. Dawn is the first type, as you probably saw."

"Do people ever mistake them for bottle-nosed dolphins?" Jody asked, remembering Dawn's slender beak.

"Sometimes," replied Brice. "But only at first glance. Because when you get up close, you can see how different their shape and coloring are from the bottle-nosed dolphins. They come in pink or gray or various shades in between. There's even a colony in Hong Kong that is almost completely white!"

Jody was intrigued. "Do they like people?"

"They aren't that sociable as a rule," said Brice. "They don't like boats and are much slower in the water than bottle-nosed dolphins, so they don't tend to bow-ride."

"But Dawn came in really close to the shore," Jody pointed out. "And she wasn't afraid of me. You saw her — she was almost as near to me as you are now!"

"Humpbacked dolphins always feed in shallow water, so they know about people and coastal development," explained Brice. "But strangely, they are well known for being difficult to approach. I think Dawn is the exception to the rule. She's a big fan of the tourists." He paused. "In fact," he added slowly, "sometimes I think she likes tourists a little too much."

Jody was surprised. "In what way?"

Brice looked thoughtful. "She's a regular at Oceans Point, and I've noticed that she's been putting on weight. It wouldn't surprise me if she was finding food somewhere she shouldn't."

"Where?"

Brice swept out a strong, tanned arm, indicating the coastline. "This part of Queensland has plenty of tourist resorts," he said. "Some of them actively encourage dolphins to swim in to shore to interact with visitors."

Jody couldn't believe her ears. "Wild dolphins?" she asked.

"Technically wild," said Brice with a frown. "But increasingly reliant on handouts. It's not something we encourage at Oceans Point." He smiled at her. "As you've just seen."

"Who's your friend, Jody?" Gina approached them, flip-flops in hand.

Jody waved her dad over as well and made some introductions. As ever, Craig and Gina were happy to meet a fellow dolphin enthusiast and were soon eagerly discussing their worldwide project with Brice. Jody left the adults to chat for a while. She walked over to her brothers, who were scuffling in the sand.

"So how many disasters have you two caused so far?" she asked.

Jimmy looked indignant. "Apart from splashing that family over there and kicking sand in that lady's picnic by mistake, we've been really good," he declared.

"And you hit that man with the Frisbee," Sean pointed out.

"Only because you said I wouldn't be able to," Jimmy protested.

Craig moved away from Gina and Brice and came toward them. "They've tired me out, anyway, I can tell you." He smiled, putting Sean in a friendly headlock. "How was the sea?"

"Great!" Jody enthused. "And I saw a dolphin!"

"So I heard." Craig looked amused. "They always seem to know when you're around, Jody!"

Jody told him all about her close-up experience with Dawn.

"I haven't seen an Indo-Pacific humpbacked dolphin for years," said Craig thoughtfully. "I'd like to take a look. Brice told me that several feed in these waters."

"Maybe she'll come back again," Jody said hopefully.

"Let's hope so," Craig said. "Brice said that she was a regular." He released Sean and clapped his hands. "Come on, guys. Our new friend Brice here has invited us back to HQ, to tell us a bit more about the resort and Hervey Bay."

Jody shaded her eyes and checked the position of the sun. It was getting quite high. She knew that staying outside in the middle of the day wasn't a good idea. A quick trip to Brice's cool, shady office would be very welcome.

"Coming?" Craig asked.

"Will there be ice cream?" asked Jimmy cunningly.

"Maybe," said Craig. "But only if you pack up your beach things in exactly ten seconds flat!"

Craig, Gina, Brice, Jody, and the boys made their way down to the waterfront. They could see Brittany still sunbathing on the rock at the far end of the tidebreak.

"Brittany!" called Gina. "We're going into town. I'd rather not leave you here on your own, so you'd better come with us. We'll come back to the beach later."

Brittany sat up and adjusted her sunglasses. Even at this distance, Jody could tell that she wasn't very pleased to be disturbed.

"I want to stay here!" she complained. "I'm just starting to get a tan. Anyway, if I go now, I'll lose this sunbathing place."

"Brittany sweetheart, we haven't got time to argue —" Gina began.

"I'm not a baby," Brittany interrupted hotly. "I can look after myself, you know."

"We can stay with Brittany," Maddie offered, wading out and shaking the water from her ears. "Cam's not going anywhere, either. Look at him!" She pointed at the figure fast asleep on a brightly colored float, which was bobbing gently in the shallows.

"Thanks, Maddie," said Gina gratefully. "Just try to get

Brittany into the shade sometime soon. It's getting close to eleven o'clock, and I don't want her coming down with heatstroke."

Jody saw her mother look at the jagged rocks of the tidebreak.

"And could you keep an eye on her if she goes anywhere near those rocks?" Gina added. "If Brittany slips and falls in, it could be nasty."

"She'll be fine," Maddie insisted. "Go and have fun! We'll see you later."

The Oceans Point wardens' office was a whitewashed wooden hut at the far end of the harbor. It stood just above a small jetty, where a gleaming launch boat, called *Kookaburra,* lay at a mooring.

Brice unlocked the office door and ushered everyone into the shady interior. A fan was whirring energetically on the wall, filling the room with a welcome breeze. "My boss is over on Fraser Island today with a four-wheel-drive tour," he explained. "But I know he'd love to meet you sometime."

"We'd like that," said Craig. "The four-wheel-drive

What a boat!

tour sounds like fun, too. Do you have many activities around here?"

"Lots." Brice laughed. "As well as the four-wheel-drive tour, there are sailing trips, fishing trips, and motorbikes."

Jimmy and Sean looked up from their melting chocolate cones at the mention of motorbikes.

"Everything is carefully monitored, though," Brice continued. "We don't want to ruin the natural environment. There aren't many places left like Hervey Bay and Fraser Island, so we've got to look after them."

Brice quickly fell into a long and detailed conversation about the environmental projects of Hervey Bay and Fraser Island with Craig and Gina, leaving Jody to keep an eye on her brothers. They had now finished their ice-cream cones and were looking for new distractions.

"Check this out!" Jimmy pointed at a glossy poster of Pacific marine life that was pinned to the office wall.

"Cool," Sean agreed, peering closely.

"I've got an idea," said Jody. "I'll give you two minutes to stare at this poster, then I'll ask you to write down the names of all the animals you can remember. The person who remembers the most wins, OK?"

Jimmy cocked his head. "Wins what?"

"The best prize in the world," said Jody. "The pleasure of beating your brother and then bragging about it for a few days."

"Excellent!" shouted Sean.

While her brothers were memorizing the poster, Jody read the flyer pinned up next to it. It was all about the history of Hervey Bay. The bay had been discovered by Captain Cook while traveling down the east coast of Australia, and he'd named it after his boss, Lord Augustus Hervey. He hadn't been very thorough, Jody decided. He'd called it Hervey *Bay* because he'd thought Fraser Island was joined to the mainland. She traced the outline of Fraser Island on the large wall map next to the office door. If Captain Cook had traveled a little farther south, he'd have discovered the narrow strait of water that separates Fraser Island from the rest of Australia.

Jody checked her watch. "OK, time's up!" she said to the twins. "Let's ask Brice for some paper and a couple of pens."

Jody's parents and Brice stopped their conversation, and Brice found something for the boys to write on. Soon Jimmy and Sean's chatter gave way to the sound of busy scribbling.

"You're good at entertaining your brothers," Brice commented, smiling at Jody.

"They've been running around the beach all morning, so getting them to sit still now is easy," said Jody. "There isn't any room on board *Dolphin Dreamer* for running around, so it's much harder keeping them out of trouble then."

"They love it here," said Gina, joining in the conversation. "Oceans Point gives them plenty of space — and gives the rest of us a break!"

"Kids sometimes find Oceans Point too quiet," Brice said. "Families often prefer the amusement parks and carnivals of the resorts farther south."

"You said something about the resorts in the south earlier," said Jody, remembering.

Brice nodded. "Yes, as I said, there are quite a few. Parts of the coast are getting pretty overdeveloped now."

"Is that a problem for the wildlife?" Craig asked with a frown.

"It used to be pretty bad in the past," said Brice. "You heard about tourists encouraging dolphins to swim close to shore, where they would beach themselves and then be unable to get back into the sea. Because of too much uncontrolled human contact, some dolphins would stop feeding their own young and become unusually aggressive. I even heard of dolphins catching human diseases."

"That's horrible," said Jody with feeling. She thought of Dawn.

"You can see why I'm worried about Dawn," Brice said, reading Jody's expression. "The only good news is that overexploitation is much less common than it used to be. These days, we keep accurate records of visiting marine life, so we can pinpoint problems pretty quickly. We also do whale-watching boat trips in season and trips out to the sea grass meadows and into deeper waters the rest of the year. We prefer to take the visitors to the wildlife, not the other way around. That takes some of the pressure off the coastline and discourages dolphins from coming too close to shore."

He pointed outside, toward the wooden jetty. "You probably saw our tour boat, *Kookaburra,* moored out there. And there are other places like Oceans Point along this coast that operate on similar principles."

He paused. "But on the other hand, there are still places along this coast with serious problems," he admitted. "If we could keep the dolphins at Oceans Point, we'd be able to protect them. But they are wild creatures, and we don't believe in penning them in."

Jody jumped at a sudden crash in the corner of the office. She swung around.

"Jimmy!" cried Gina, throwing her hands in the air.

Jimmy stood next to the overturned office chair, whose wheels were gently spinning in the air. A wastepaper bin also lay on its side, spilling a fluttering heap of paper across the floor.

"It was Sean," he said unconvincingly.

"I think we'd better take the boys back to *Dolphin Dreamer,*" Craig apologized to Brice. "Before they break something."

Brice laughed. "But I haven't shown you *Kookaburra* yet!" he said. "Maybe you'd like to come out on a trip this afternoon?"

"We'd love to!" Jody said enthusiastically. She had totally fallen in love with this place and couldn't wait to explore it further. "Dad, can we?"

"I don't see why not —" Craig began.

There was another crash as the office door flew open, letting in a flood of light. Maddie stood framed in the doorway.

"Is Brittany here with you?" she asked urgently.

There was a pause.

"We left her with you!" Gina exclaimed.

Maddie looked anxious. "I know. One minute she was there, and the next she was gone. If she isn't here with you, where could she have gone? I've looked everywhere for her."

"Did you check *Dolphin Dreamer*?" asked Craig.

Maddie nodded unhappily. "Harry hadn't seen her. He's out looking for her on the beach now."

"We'd better join the hunt," said Gina. "Brice, it's been a pleasure talking to you. Now we'd better go and find Brittany."

4

"Don't worry, Gina," said Maddie. "Wherever Brittany is, I'm sure she's fine. She took her towel with her, so she must have wandered off somewhere on purpose."

"She should have said something to you." Gina sighed, passing a hand over her forehead. "Now we'll have to spend ages looking for her, and I know Mei Lin is expecting us back on board for lunch soon. This is supposed to be a vacation!"

"I'm sure you'll find her," said Brice reassuringly,

locking the office door behind him. "Why don't you come back after lunch? I meant what I said about showing you *Kookaburra*. We've got a tour at two o'clock, if you're interested. Maybe I'll see you later?"

"Thanks." Gina nodded. "If we can make it, that would be great."

There was no sign of Brittany at the beach.

"You two go that way," Craig instructed Maddie and Cam, pointing away from the harbor front. "We'll check out the harbor. Let's meet back at the jetty in half an hour, OK?"

Jody went with her parents to the harbor front, where they asked every passerby whether they'd seen a girl on her own with wavy blond hair and pink flip-flops.

"We'll check inside the shops, and you stay out here, Jody," Gina said at last. "She must be around somewhere. We'll see you at the jetty."

Several times, Jody thought she'd spotted Brittany in the crowd, but it always turned out to be someone else. With a sigh, she turned her attention to the small waterfront café on the harbor front.

Jody suddenly spotted Dr. Taylor sitting at one of the café tables.

Dr. Taylor looked a little embarrassed. "Uh, hello, Jody," he said, pushing his large ice-cream sundae to one side. "Just a quick break, here." He patted a small pile of flyers on the table. "Research is thirsty work," he added jovially. "Now, is something the matter?"

Jody explained about Brittany. Dr. Taylor nodded carefully. "Yes," he said at last. "That doesn't surprise me. She certainly is a willful young lady."

"Have you seen her?" Jody persisted.

Dr. Taylor shook his head. "No," he admitted. "I've been reading these flyers, you see. One hundred percent concentration needed!"

"There you are, Dr. Taylor!" Jody heard Mei Lin's voice and turned around to see the slender Chinese woman standing with her arms full of grocery bags. "Are you ready to go back to the boat? There are several more of these to pick up," she added meaningfully, indicating the small mini-market a hundred yards away.

Dr. Taylor grumbled under his breath before heading in the direction Mei Lin was pointing.

"Mei Lin, have you seen Brittany?" Jody asked hopefully.

Mei Lin shook her head. "I know Maddie was looking for her earlier, because she came back to *Dolphin Dreamer* and told us," she said. "So you still haven't found her?"

Jody shook her head.

"Don't worry," said Mei Lin comfortingly, hefting her groceries into a better position. "It's nearly twelve o'clock. Brittany won't miss lunch! I'll see you back at the boat in no time."

After half an hour, Jody gave up and started hurrying back to the jetty to meet the others.

"So that's why it's called Hervey Bay. . . ."

Jody stopped as she heard a very familiar voice behind her.

"Brittany!" Jody swung around in relief to see Brittany strolling along with a tall, tanned boy in sunglasses. "There you are! We've been looking everywhere for you!"

"Why? What's all the fuss?" Brittany looked perplexed. She turned to her companion. "I just met Jason here, and we got to talking."

Gina and Craig came running up. "There you are!" cried Gina in relief. "Brittany, where on earth have you been?"

Brittany looked mutinous. "This is Jason. He and I met at the harbor front, and we started talking, and . . ." she said.

"You should have told Maddie or Cam where you were," Craig interrupted, annoyed. "We've been worried sick."

Brittany rolled her eyes. "It's my vacation, too. I am thirteen, you know. Mom always let me go off on my own."

"Still, you should have told someone where you were going," Craig repeated. He turned to Jason. "Will you excuse us? Brittany has some explaining to do."

Jason shrugged. "No worries," he said, before walking off toward the beach.

Brittany glared. "That was so embarrassing," she muttered.

"Embarrassment is the least of your problems," said

Craig severely. "I think your dad might have something to say about this. It's time to head back to *Dolphin Dreamer* for lunch."

He paused, looking at Brittany's face. "And by the way," he added grimly, "your nose is peeling."

March 15 — lunchtime

Brittany has shut herself in our cabin and is refusing to speak to anyone. I think it's partly because she's sulking and partly because she doesn't want anyone to see her peeling nose. She didn't have enough sunscreen on after all. I suppose you can't really blame her for wanting to do her own thing. I think her big mistake was not telling anyone where she was going.

Now that we've found her, it means that we can go back to the wardens' office after lunch for a deep-sea tour aboard Kookaburra*! Maybe we'll see Dawn again. Even if we don't, I know we're going to see some amazing things.*

Lunch was fantastic. As Jody sank her teeth into fresh, juicy tomatoes and crunched through crisp salad leaves, she thought she'd gone to heaven.

"How did old-time sailors survive whole *months* at sea?" she asked Harry as she bit hungrily into another fluffy poppy-seed roll.

Harry laughed. "With great difficulty," he joked. "I'm pleased to say that I've never been at sea for more than a couple of months at a time, so I've never had the pleasure of weevil-infested bread and rotten meat."

"Yuck!" said Jimmy. "Did they have to eat the ship's rats, too?"

Jody noticed that Brittany wasn't eating very much. She was picking quietly at a roll and staring at the deck. Jody guessed that Harry had said a few harsh words to his daughter when they'd gotten back on board.

"More cheese, Brittany?" Gina gently offered Brittany the plate. "Mei Lin found some wonderful fresh soft cheese for us."

Brittany pushed her chair back. "I'm sorry, OK?" she blurted out. "I should have told you where I was going. I was just . . ." She paused, struggling for words. "I just needed to get away from everyone for a while. . . ." She stopped abruptly.

Craig put his hand on her shoulder. Brittany always

47

found apologizing very hard to do. "That's OK," he said quietly. "Don't worry about it."

Brittany looked across at Jody, her eyes brimming with tears. "Is my nose really bad?" she asked in a watery voice.

Jody thought Brittany's nose was redder than the tomato on her plate, but she wasn't going to say that. "No," she lied. "It'll be fine. Just put lots of moisturizer on it and stay out of the sun for a while."

Brittany sniffed and picked up the remains of her roll. She didn't say another word at lunch, and as soon as the plates were cleared, she disappeared into her cabin.

"Isn't Brittany coming with us on the *Kookaburra* tour?" Jody asked, watching Brittany go.

"She's feeling a little sorry for herself today," said Harry, folding away the lunch table and stowing it neatly. "I think she just needs some time. I'm sure she'd love to hear about it later, Jody."

"So you'll have to remember all the smallest details for her," Gina advised.

"I'll remember those, anyway," Jody said honestly.

"Shame you don't remember your math formulas quite so easily!" remarked Maddie with a grin.

Jody, her brothers, and her parents made their way to the Oceans Point wardens' office at a quarter to two. Brice was waiting for them.

On closer inspection, *Kookaburra* turned out to be a catamaran with a special glass floor, so visitors could see under the water. Even moored at the jetty, Jody was enthralled by the view through the glass. She could see seaweed waving on the ocean bed and shells on the seabed floor.

Kookaburra was painted blue and white and built on three levels. There was a sea-level viewing platform, with the glass floor inside and an open deck at the front of the boat. The second level was completely covered, allowing viewing and seating, and finally there was the cockpit at the top. Jody and the twins explored every inch, delighting at the framed pictures of whales and dolphins on the walls and the twisting stairways that took them from level to level.

"Hey!" a timid voice called from the jetty. "Is anyone aboard?"

Jody ran out on deck. "Brittany!" she said in delight. "You came!"

Brittany stood sheepishly on the jetty, clutching a small beach bag. She was wearing a large floppy sun hat, and her nose was liberally coated in white sunblock. She twisted her hair around her fingers. "Can I come on the tour?" she asked tentatively.

Brittany tries to make amends

"Of course you can, honey," said Gina warmly, holding out her hand to help Brittany step aboard. "Good to have you with us."

Brittany immediately wanted to go right to the top deck.

"There's not much to see up here," Jody said when they got there. "Wait till you see *Kookaburra*'s glass bottom — it's amazing!"

Brittany slowly looked around the tiny top deck. "I like it up here," she said. "I want to look at the view." She leaned on the rail and gazed back toward the harbor and the beach.

Something about the expression on Brittany's face made Jody wonder if she was looking for someone. "Did that boy say he was coming on the tour?" Jody said, with a sudden flash of inspiration.

Brittany flushed a dark red. "He may have," she said in a careless voice. "I can't remember."

"Who are you talking about?" Jimmy poked his head up the steps.

Brittany stared desperately at Jody. She obviously didn't want Jody to say anything about the boy at the beach.

"About Brice," Jody said.

Jimmy shrugged, bored with the conversation already. "Sean just saw an octopus through the glass bottom of the boat," he declared, and disappeared down the steps again.

"Thanks, Jody," said Brittany gratefully. "I owe you one. If Jimmy knew I'd been talking to a boy, he'd only make a big thing of it." She looked across at the beach again.

"Is that him?" asked Jody suddenly.

A tall boy was walking down the jetty, toward the boat.

"Yes!" Brittany squealed, turning red again. She swung around to Jody anxiously. "My nose doesn't look too awful, does it?"

"Aussies always wear stripes of sunblock on their noses," Jody said generously. "I'm sure Jason will think it's cool."

At two o'clock exactly, *Kookaburra* pulled away from the jetty and headed out into the open sea. Brittany and Jason had immediately started talking, and now they were sitting at the front of the boat with their heads together.

"Welcome aboard the *Kookaburra*, folks." Brice's voice sounded over a loudspeaker. "Let's go see what Hervey Bay has to offer!"

The next hour passed like a dream for Jody. She stood at the bow, holding on tightly to the rail. It wasn't long before the first dolphins made an appearance, leaping high off to starboard.

"Bottle-nosed dolphins are quite common in these parts," Brice stated. "But you need to keep your eyes peeled for their shier cousins, the Indo-Pacific hump-backed dolphin. We have some visitors aboard who know more about dolphins than I do, and I'm sure they'll be happy to answer your questions — Craig and Gina McGrath, from Florida!"

The other tourists looked curiously at Craig and Gina, and Jody felt a stab of pride.

Pelicans came into view, flying in low, ungainly swoops along the water. The baggy sacs in their bills meant that they could scoop unsuspecting fish clean out of the water and either swallow them right away or save some for later.

"These waters are teeming with fish, as you might

expect," Brice continued as *Kookaburra* began to leave the deep water behind and head for the shore of Fraser Island. "Species include snapper, coral trout, bream, sweetlip, and trevally, plus others such as tuna, mackerel, and marlin. All good feeding for our friends the pelicans and the ospreys that nest on the mainland."

Jody saw a humpback shape break the surface of the water briefly, then disappear. She turned to Brittany. "Did you see that?" she said in excitement.

Brittany looked up from her conversation with Jason. "See what?" she said.

"I'm sure that was a humpbacked dolphin," explained Jody, turning back to the sea again. *Maybe it was Dawn,* she thought. She craned her neck in case the dolphin reappeared, but there was no sign of it.

Brice brought the *Kookaburra* about half a mile from the shore of Fraser Island and dropped anchor in the clear waters of a sheltered bay. The sandy, tree-tangled shore looked wild and uninhabited, but the waters were quite the opposite. The water here was perfectly clear with a light aqua tinge. Jody could see different shapes and colors as a large turtle swam past and small fish darted around in the shallows.

"It's a bird!" Brittany cried in astonishment as a gliding shadow seemed to fly along beneath them, beating strong wings.

Sean and Jimmy laughed.

"That's a manta ray, Brittany," Gina said gently. "Though to be fair, it does look like a bird when it glides along like that."

"I thought it was some kind of bird, too," said Jason gallantly.

Brittany blushed and put some more sunblock on her nose.

Jody could see a gently moving seabed of what looked like green meadow grass, swaying in the current.

"These are the sea grass meadows," Brice announced. "There aren't many left, so it's up to us to preserve and look after them. They're a very important feeding ground for an endangered species. If we're very lucky, we should see this species. Now be quiet and watch."

Jody wasn't sure what they were watching for. But she dutifully stared down into the pale water and waited.

Suddenly, she gave a shout. "Someone's down there! Someone's fallen overboard!"

5

Brice raced up beside Jody. "Where?" he asked urgently.

Jody pointed down into the water with a shaking hand. Whoever it was wasn't moving. Were they dead already?

Brice stared down into the water. Then he burst out laughing.

"It's OK, folks," he called back to the other tourists, who had gathered around the edge of the boat. "No one's in danger. In fact, what we're looking at here is a wonderful sight. Someone having a hearty meal!"

Jody stared. The "person" had started moving. It changed position and brought its head down to the sea grass, where it calmly began to graze.

"What is it?" asked Brittany, hanging back fearfully.

"It's a dugong," replied Craig, putting his hand on Jody's shoulder.

A dugong? Jody remembered reading about dugongs when she had first looked at the Hervey Bay web site. Her heart stopped racing, and she started feeling embarrassed.

"Sailors used to mistake dugongs for humans," Brice said kindly. "Well," he amended, "not humans exactly. But sirens, or mermaids."

"Mermaids?" Jimmy echoed, peering over the edge of the boat. "That's a seriously ugly mermaid!"

The dugong wasn't the prettiest creature Jody had ever seen. It was enormous, with a wrinkled hide and heavy, powerful flippers. Its snout was blunt and whiskered. Jody watched as it rooted gently along the seabed, tearing up the sea grass and munching slowly.

"Because they feed almost exclusively on sea grass, they're also known as sea cows," explained Brice.

"Cow is a bit more realistic than mermaid." Brittany snorted. "Those sailors must have been at sea for a long time!"

Brice smiled. "Mermaids were said to lure ships onto dangerous rocks and drive men mad with their seductive songs. The sailors were probably too superstitious to look too closely. When you'd been at sea for several months, your water and your food was low. If your ship was straying dangerously close to the shore, maybe you'd think these creatures were mermaids, too."

Brittany tossed her head. "As if!" she said scornfully.

"I think they're pretty cool," said Jason.

"I'm not saying they aren't *cool*," said Brittany, glancing at Jason. "They just aren't mermaids, that's all."

Jody leaned farther over the rail and squinted down into the glittering water to get a better look at the dugong. "How big do they grow?" she asked.

"This one's a young male — he looks about two and a half yards long. But they can grow up to three yards," Brice said. "That's roughly twice the height of your mom."

Jody glanced across at her mother, who was deep in

conversation with an American couple on the deck. The image of a dugong standing on its tail and towering over Gina made her smile.

"They can live for a long time, about seventy years or so." Brice leaned on *Kookaburra*'s railing and watched the dugong as it grazed peacefully below them. "But they don't start breeding until the females are roughly ten to seventeen years old. They only have one calf every three to five years, and pregnancy lasts thirteen months. So the population doesn't increase as fast as we'd like it to."

"You said they were an endangered species," Jody recalled aloud. "Is that because they don't breed fast enough?"

"Partly that," said Brice. "But mainly because there aren't many sea grass meadows left. When you think that a full-grown adult dugong will eat around fifty-five pounds of sea grass a day, that's a whole lot of food. Maintaining the sea grass meadows is one of the main projects we have in Hervey Bay. If we don't look after the meadows, we'll lose these amazing creatures for good."

As she talked to Brice, Jody learned more about dugongs. Although they looked like very heavy dolphins or seals, their closest relative was the elephant. And unlike dolphins or whales, they couldn't hold their breath for much longer than fifteen minutes at a time — or less, if they were swimming fast.

"So we should see this one surface?" Jody asked hopefully.

Brice nodded. "Yes. Unless he chooses to swim farther away from the boat before he takes a breath."

There was a shout from the other side of the boat. Dolphins!

"There's a group of four just to the seaward side of us," Gina said as soon as Jody had joined them. She pointed, and Jody squinted. Four dorsal fins rose and fell through the surface of the glittering water, before all four dolphins leaped into the air in perfect synchronicity.

"Bottle-nosed dolphins again," said Jody immediately, her heart lifting as it always did. "I think I saw that humpbacked dolphin again earlier," she added. "The one I saw at the beach — Dawn."

"Are you sure?" said Gina, frowning. "Brice said they were a pretty rare sighting. It's unlikely that you'd see the same one twice in one day, don't you think?"

Jody felt disappointed that her mother thought it was unlikely. She really wanted her parents to see the wonderful creature. The only person who had seen Dawn except for Jody was Brice. It felt very strange, being the only one in her family who knew what Dawn looked like.

She walked back across the deck to see if the dugong was still there. But the sea grass meadow was still and quiet. The dugong had moved on. Jody took the opportunity to take out her diary for a moment.

March 15 — afternoon — sitting on the deck of Kookaburra
I felt pretty stupid right now. I thought someone had fallen overboard on the Kookaburra *tour. I could see this figure sitting on the seabed, and I couldn't see any scuba equipment. I wondered if they'd gotten themselves tangled in the sea grass or something and couldn't come up to breathe. It's true that I didn't exactly hear or see any-*

one fall overboard. But it looked so real! So I yelled my head off. Well, what would you have done?

I'm sure Dawn was following Kookaburra. I know Mom thought I was imagining things, but I felt her there. I don't know how else to explain it. I know I think about dolphins a lot, but I'm pretty sure I don't imagine them.

The squawk of an unfamiliar bird made Jody look up from the page. The *Kookaburra* moved closer to the shore of Fraser Island, where they could swim. The breakers along the shore were gentle and lazy — one of the benefits of a shoreline that faced mainland Australia and not the endless Pacific Ocean.

Jimmy and Sean wasted no time in stripping down to their trunks and leaping into the inviting water. Craig and Gina joined them, and one by one most of the other *Kookaburra* passengers lowered themselves overboard as well. Jody put away her diary and sat at the prow of the boat, swinging her legs and deciding whether or not to go in. Part of her wanted to stay on the boat and keep watch on the horizon, in case Dawn returned. But the rest of her knew that the water would be nice and cool.

"Come on, Brittany — let's go for a swim."

Jody looked around to see Jason trying to coax Brittany over the side of the boat.

"Oh, no." Brittany shook her head vigorously. "I'm not going in there. I'm staying right here, OK?"

Jason shrugged. "Suit yourself." He jumped overboard into the clear blue waves, one knee curled up underneath him for maximum splash. Then he struck off toward the twins, who were playing tag.

Jody thought it looked like fun and prepared to jump in as well. "You normally love swimming," she said to Brittany curiously. "Don't you want to come in?"

Brittany rolled her eyes. "Don't you know anything, Jody?" she said fussily. "Seawater is the worst thing for your hair. If it goes frizzy today, I'll just die." She took off her sun hat and smoothed down her hair. "I'm going inside for a while, to check out this glass bottom you were raving about earlier," she said. "Hope it's as good as you said it was."

Jody plunged down into the inviting water and

swam over toward Sean, Jimmy, and Jason. Within minutes, she was breathless and laughing, shaking water from her ears and eyes and trying to hold on to her slippery little brothers as they raced past.

Soon the boys were tired, and they all began to make their way back to *Kookaburra*. The adults were already back on board, talking and laughing in the afternoon sunshine.

Jason paddled up to Jody. "It's a shame Brittany didn't want to come in," he said. "She's kind of fun. You're not sisters, are you?"

Jody shook her head and explained how Brittany had come to join their expedition.

"Whoa. That's tough," said Jason sympathetically. He looked back at the boat.

Jody knew he was wondering why Brittany hadn't come swimming. She couldn't tell him about Brittany's hair, because she knew Brittany would be mad.

"Brittany's a hard person to understand sometimes," she said in the end. "She said she wanted to check out the glass bottom of the boat, but I think she just wanted to be on her own for a while, you know?"

Suddenly, Jason's eyes brightened. "Hey! I've just had a great idea!" he said, beckoning Jody closer. "Listen to this! Brittany's going to love it."

He whispered something in Jody's ear.

"You're not serious!" Jody cried.

"Are we on, or not?" Jason insisted.

Jody shook her head firmly. Then she opened her mouth. "Yes," she found herself saying, to her astonishment. "Why not?"

Jason grinned. "Follow me."

Jody swam after Jason as he quietly approached the side of *Kookaburra.* "Are you ready?" he asked.

Jody nodded. "On the count of three," she said. "One, two, three, GO!"

Jody took a deep breath and sank down under the water. She followed Jason toward the hull of *Kookaburra.* With a swift kick of her legs, she ducked right underneath the hull — and swam beneath the glass bottom of the boat. A few moments later, she popped up again and took a huge gasping breath. Jason popped up beside her.

On the count of three . . .

"Did you see her?" he asked eagerly.

Jody shook her head. "I was too busy trying to get to the other side! What about you?"

"Well . . ." Jason began.

Suddenly, Jody could hear someone screaming on board the *Kookaburra*.

She looked across at Jason. "I guess Brittany saw us," she said, with a sinking feeling.

They both swam quietly up to the boat and scrambled up the ladder onto the deck. Jody could hear her mother's voice deep inside the cabin.

"Of course it wasn't a mermaid, sweetheart," Gina was saying. "You heard what Brice was saying about the sailors getting mistaken. It must have been a dugong."

"It had hair!" Brittany was wailing. "Long dark hair that waved behind it like seaweed! It wasn't a dugong, Aunt Gina — honest!"

"Did it have a fish tail?" Sean asked with interest.

Jody tugged on Jason's sleeve with a sigh. "Come on," she said. "We'd better go and explain. But I warn you — it's not going to be pretty."

It was time to head back to Oceans Point. Brittany had disappeared up to the cockpit with Brice and was refusing to come down, even though Jody and Jason had both apologized over and over again. Jason was sitting glumly at the prow of the boat, and Jimmy and Sean were running around the deck doing impressions of Brittany, screeching, "It's a mermaid! It's a mermaid!" Jody felt really bad about it. If there was one thing Brittany hated more than looking stupid, it was looking stupid in front of a boy.

"You've really done it this time," Gina said, hands on her hips. Jody thought she saw a slight smirk cross her mother's face.

"I know. I'm sorry," Jody said. "I didn't think Brittany would mistake me for a mermaid — I just thought it would be funny to wave at her when we swam under the boat. But I guess I forgot the waving part."

Gina looked up at the cockpit. "I suppose she'll get over it," she said with a sigh. "Eventually."

Brice's voice floated down from the cockpit. "In case you are interested after our rather exciting afternoon, I have a little treat for you as we leave Fraser Island today. If you look to your left, you'll see a couple of friendly faces."

Jody looked — and gasped. The round, bronze-colored head of a dugong was poking up above the water level, flaring its wide nostrils and snorting gently at the air. Beside the dugong was the smaller head of a calf, doing the same as its mother. Jody couldn't quite believe her eyes, but it looked as if the mother dugong was cradling the calf between her flippers, just like a human mother with a child.

"Your eyes aren't deceiving you," Brice said through the loudspeaker. "Dugongs do sit upright and hold their calves with their flippers, allowing the youngsters to nurse just like a human child would. We are very honored to see one of the most loving sights in the animal kingdom. Let's do what we can to preserve these wonderful creatures. Now — time to head for home."

March 15 — evening — back on the jetty at Oceans Point after supper (fresh sausages!)

I don't know what came over me earlier today. It was pretty funny, but it kind of backfired. Brittany is refusing to speak to me and is in with her dad right now, asking to be moved to a different cabin. Unless she wants to sleep on deck, there's nowhere else for her to go, so I guess I'm just going to suffer the silent treatment tonight — and maybe for the next few days, too. Jason is history. B told him that she never wants to speak to him again, either. Mom scolded me, but I think she saw the funny side. I feel bad for giving B such a fright, but we honestly didn't mean to. I should know by now that she's not very good at taking a joke!

Jody put down her diary and stretched out her legs in the cool evening air. Broken reflections of the low moon danced on the water, and she felt really lucky to be discovering more and more of the fascinating wildlife beneath the waves.

6

March 16 — after lunch — Oceans Point harbor
It's so beautiful and peaceful here. We've just been lazing around on the beach and checking out the harbor-front cafés today. Maddie, Cam, and Mei Lin thought the Kook-aburra tour sounded so great that they've headed off to do it this afternoon. Mom, Dad, the twins, and I are at the café now, where we've just had a fantastic lunch of fresh grilled fish. Dad and the boys just shared a huge ice-cream sundae that was almost as big as Jimmy and Sean put together!

Because Brittany's still pretty mad, she's done the op-

posite of us all morning. So when we were at the beach, she was at the café, and the other way around. She's back on board Dolphin Dreamer *now. She's wearing big dark glasses in case she sees Jason — I don't think she wants him to recognize her.*

The coastline stretches up to a small headland a little way south of here. I wonder what's on the other side. I might ask Dad if we can do some exploring this afternoon. Harry's been adjusting the tension on Dolphin Dreamer's *sails, and I think he'd like to try them out. Also, there's been no sign of Dawn this morning. Maybe she's moved on down the coast.*

Jody closed her diary thoughtfully and took another sip of her vanilla milk shake. If Dawn had moved farther down the coast, maybe they wouldn't see her again. The thought upset her. She'd seen Dawn for only a few brief moments, but she knew there was something very special about her. Plus, she knew her parents would love to see the humpbacked dolphin. It would be such a shame if they never did.

Craig pushed back his chair. "Well," he said, "I don't

know about you guys, but I'm full to bursting here. That sundae finished me off."

Gina laughed. "You didn't have to have it, Craig," she teased.

Craig shrugged with a twinkle in his eye. "I know. But I'm on vacation!" he said.

Jody looked toward *Dolphin Dreamer,* which was bobbing quietly at its mooring.

"Dad," she said, "do you think we could take *Dolphin Dreamer* down the coast today?"

"Cool!" said Jimmy and Sean together.

Craig took off his sunglasses and polished them on the hem of his shirt. "I don't see why not," he said after a moment. "If Harry's up to it, it might be nice to do some exploring. I know Cam's with the *Kookaburra* this afternoon, but we can all lend Harry a hand. Let's talk to him when we get back to the boat, OK?"

"What are we going to do about Brittany?" said Gina. "We ought to ask her to come along as well."

Jody frowned. She hadn't really thought about that. She knew their argument would blow over eventually, but Brittany was so unpredictable.

Jimmy and Sean groaned and rolled back in their chairs.

"She'll just complain all the time if she comes," said Jimmy.

"Can't we leave her here?" Sean added.

Gina stood up from the café table. "No," she said in a decided voice. "She's had all morning to herself, and I think it's time that she talked to us. We'll ask her very nicely, and Jody will apologize again. Then we can get back to normal."

Jody opened her mouth to say that she didn't think Brittany would listen. But Gina held up her hand.

"I know you've apologized several times already, Jody," she said gently. "But Brittany will have to give in eventually. Why don't you buy her something from one of the shops here and take it back to the boat? As a peace offering."

Jody looked along the harbor front. There was one shop that sold trinkets and souvenirs. She might be able to find something.

"OK," she agreed. She still had about five Australian

dollars left over from the money her dad had given her that morning.

Gina looked relieved. "Good girl," she said. "It's time we got this vacation back on a friendly footing. We'll head back to the boat and discuss the idea of a short trip with Harry, OK?"

Jody wandered along the harbor front after her family left. There wasn't much in the souvenir shop. Oceans Point was definitely a nature reserve, not a vacation resort. Giving up after about twenty minutes, she wandered down to the beach. She walked along the shore, kicking the little breakers that bubbled gently over her feet. What could she get for Brittany?

"Jody?" It was Jason, looking a little anxious and slightly out of breath. "I saw you from over there," he said, pointing toward the trees.

"Hi, Jason." Jody smiled.

Jason shuffled his feet in the sand. "Is Brittany OK?"

Jody made a face. "She's still in a bad mood," she said. "We all want to go on a coast cruise in *Dolphin Dreamer* this afternoon, but we have to cheer her up first. Got any ideas for a good present?" she added hopefully.

Jason grinned. He rummaged in his knapsack, which he had slung over his shoulder. "I was hoping to see you today," he said from the depths of his bag. "Would you give Brittany this?"

He held out a magnificent shell. "It's a nautilus," he explained. "I found it this morning. I'd like Brittany to have it. I want her to know I'm sorry."

Jody stared at the shell. It was mottled pink and white, with a wonderful curling shape and a smooth mother-of-pearl interior. She held it up to her ear and heard the whooshing sound of the sea.

"Jason, it's beautiful!" she exclaimed. "Brittany will love it. You've saved my life!"

Jason shrugged. "No worries," he said shyly. He threw his bag up over his shoulder again. "See you around."

Jody watched as Jason loped back up the beach and disappeared among the trees. Then she started running back to the harbor, clutching the precious shell.

Clattering down the jetty to reach *Dolphin Dreamer,* she saw her mother waiting for her.

"How did you make out?" asked Gina.

Jody grinned and waved the shell. "Pretty good!"

With one leap, she jumped deftly aboard the boat and ran down the steps to the cabin she shared with Brittany. Before her courage failed, she knocked on the door.

After a moment, the door opened about an inch.

"What do you want?" said Brittany sourly.

Jody leaned against the door of the cabin and caught her breath. "I saw Jason today," she said.

Brittany blushed angrily. "So?"

Jody held out the nautilus. "He wanted me to give you this and to tell you how sorry he is that he upset you. I'm sorry, too."

Brittany opened the door a little wider. She slowly took the shell and turned it over in her hands. "Does it sound like the sea when you listen to it?" she said at last.

"Yes!" said Jody, relieved. "It's amazing. Try it!"

Brittany listened. A smile twitched at her lips. "That's pretty cool," she admitted.

Jody held her breath. Was she forgiven?

"I really am sorry, Brittany," she repeated. "Can we be friends again?"

Brittany looked at the shell in her hands, turning it

around so that the light caught the beautiful mother-of-pearl shine. "OK," she said.

March 16 — afternoon — on the move!
Harry found this place called Golden Sands on the map, just south of the headland we can see. He called the harbormaster just now, so they are expecting us. It sounds like a fun place. I think it's more developed than Oceans Point, with a bigger beach and more things to do. Jimmy and Sean think there'll be video games, and Brittany can't wait to see the shops. We left a message with the harbormaster for Cam, Maddie, and Mei Lin, telling them that we'd be back by suppertime. Dr. Taylor's come with us, but I don't think he approves of this new "vacation jaunt," as he calls it!

Jody stretched her arms up high, feeling the rush of cool air against her skin. It was fun to be sailing again. Harry was keeping *Dolphin Dreamer* fairly close to the shore, so the water was still shallow and clear enough to see shoals of fish chasing one another across the seabed.

The long, low flank of Fraser Island was still visible to the left as they slowly rounded the headland. *Dolphin Dreamer*'s hull shuddered against the buffeting of the changing currents, crashing through the waves and tilting with the wind.

At last, the Golden Sands resort came into view.

"Look!" Brittany pointed eagerly at the forest of masts and sails in the Golden Sands harbor.

When they arrived at Oceans Point after four weeks at sea, it had felt like the busiest place on earth. But as they neared Golden Sands, Jody realized that it was nothing compared to the bustle of a real vacation resort. The Golden Sands seafront seemed to sprawl for more than a mile, with brightly colored shops, restaurants, and arcades all along the way. The beach sloped straight down from the seafront with the harbor tucked in the middle, neatly dividing the beach in two. As *Dolphin Dreamer* turned into the harbor, the smell of frying fish and cotton candy floated in the air and Jody could hear the unmistakable beat of loud party music. She felt very out of place suddenly, staring around at the busy scene. An image of Oceans Point came into her mind. Oh, why had she suggested coming here? She knew immediately that she hated it.

Brittany's eyes were bright. "This looks great!" she enthused as Harry steered *Dolphin Dreamer* into a mooring with the help of Craig, who had jumped onto the pontoon to catch the ropes.

"This looks ghastly," complained Dr. Taylor, shading his eyes and wrinkling his nose in disgust. "I have no idea what your parents were thinking of, agreeing to come to a place like this, Jody. It's so . . ." He searched for the word. "Brash," he finally declared.

"Well, life is all about contrasts, Dr. Taylor," said Gina, with a small frown on her face. "I admit it's not really my kind of place, either, but we're here now. So I think we should make the best of it, don't you?" She shouldered a beach bag and stepped down onto the pontoon. "We'll only be here for a couple of hours. And you may find more flyers to add to your dossier."

"I don't think anything here would provide appropriate material for my research," mused Dr. Taylor. "I shall simply stay on board and catch up on my latest correspondence with PetroCo." He glanced at the seafront again and shuddered. "Brash," he muttered again, before disappearing belowdecks.

"Here is some money for everyone to spend as they please," said Craig, handing Jody and the twins five dollars each. "But that's it," he cautioned. "I'm not handing out any more, is that clear?"

"We're going to the video games," said Sean and Jimmy immediately.

Harry pressed ten dollars into Brittany's hand. "I know that you miss the lively life sometimes, Brittany," he said apologetically. "So now's your chance to enjoy yourself."

"I want some new sunglasses," Brittany decided. "*If* I can find any for only ten dollars," she added pointedly.

"Well," said Harry after a moment, "a challenge like that is always more fun, don't you think?"

Brittany scowled, but she tucked the money carefully into her pocket, anyway.

The smell of frying and burnt sugar was much stronger now that they were ashore. There seemed to be hundreds of people browsing along the seafront, all eating dripping ice-cream cones and french fries from greasy bags. Jody found that most of them seemed to be walking toward her, and she had to push her way through the oncoming crowd. A soggy fries bag suddenly blew up and into her face and startled her. Her parents seemed miles ahead.

Jody felt a pang of longing for the peace and quiet of Oceans Point. She'd known right away that Golden Sands wasn't her kind of place, but there was something else about the resort that was making her uneasy. She saw litter blowing in the wind, swirling along the boardwalk and down onto the shoreline. People were crowded together on the beach, and the sea had a strange, oily sheen of sunscreen floating on its surface.

"There you are!" Gina exclaimed when Jody finally caught up with her family. "We thought we'd lost you."

Craig looked worried. "It's going to be very easy to get lost here," he said. "If any of you do get lost, you have to promise me now that you'll make your way back to *Dolphin Dreamer.*"

Brittany rolled her eyes. "I'm not totally dumb, you know," she said.

Jimmy and Sean promised faithfully not to get lost, then charged into the nearest arcade.

"I'll go with the boys," said Craig, checking his watch. "Shall we meet back at the boat at around four o'clock?"

Jody looked along the shoreline. Several hundred yards away, the crowds seemed to thin out a little. "I'm going to walk along the beach," she said.

"Getting away from the crowds?" Gina guessed.

Jody laughed. Her mother knew her pretty well.

Brittany shook her head. "I don't get you, Jody," she said. "We've got peace and quiet at Oceans Point. We wanted something different today, so we came to Golden Sands. Look at all these shops! I'm going to look for sunglasses. Coming, Aunt Gina?"

Jody waved good-bye and made her way down to the waterfront. She had to walk for almost fifteen minutes before she found a quieter, more secluded part of the beach. It was unlikely that she'd see any marine life. There were simply too many people around. Still, she decided it was better than all the jostling around the harbor.

Suddenly, she realized what was making her uneasy. She hadn't seen a single warden or lifeguard along the beaches or by the harbor. At Oceans Point, the wardens were easily recognized in their green polo shirts. She knew that Golden Sands wasn't a nature reserve, but Brice had made it sound as if the whole Queensland coastline was special and needed looking after. Golden Sands felt like the kind of place that might ignore this. Her sense of unease grew stronger.

She began to wade out into the water. About a hundred yards out, she was still only up to her thighs. The shallows stretched out for another half mile before the color of the water grew deeper and bluer.

Some distance to her left, she noticed a group of people standing together in the waves. They seemed to be looking at something. Shading her eyes from the sun, she stared.

It was a dolphin. Jody could hardly believe her eyes. A wild dolphin, in water as shallow as this? Wading quickly toward the crowd, she realized something else. The people were reaching out to the dolphin and touching it. Worse still, they were *feeding* it.

"Stop!" she called. "You shouldn't feed the dolphins. Please stop!"

You mustn't feed the dolphins!

The crowd was too far away to hear her, or they were just ignoring her. Jody tried to wade quicker, but the water sucked at her legs, slowing her down.

A sharp whistle behind her made her stop in her tracks. Turning around, she came face-to-face with a pink-and-white-colored dolphin, whose hump and splashed beak made her heart leap in her chest.

"Dawn!" she whispered. "Is that you?"

The humpbacked dolphin approached her. With a shiver, Jody stared into the depths of one wild, bright eye. She was sure it was Dawn! The dolphin clicked gently and nodded her beak in the air.

She wants food, Jody realized. "I don't have anything for you," she said quietly, trying not to remember all the terrible things Brice had told her about dolphins who became dependent on handouts. "You shouldn't be asking for food, Dawn! It's not good for you."

She waved her hands at the dolphin as gently as she could. She didn't want to scare her, but she had to send her back out to sea.

Dawn rolled over and dived. For one brief moment, Jody thought she had succeeded. Then she saw Dawn resurface — right next to the group of tourists Jody had been trying to approach.

With a dull feeling of inevitability, Jody watched one of the tourists reach out toward Dawn, offering her one of his french fries. A burst of laughter floated across the water.

"Don't you realize what you're doing?" Jody called across the water. "It's wrong to feed dolphins!"

One of the tourists turned and stared at her. He was young, with sunburned shoulders and a stripe of pink sunblock across his nose.

"But it's hungry," he called back. "We're not doing any harm. Why don't you go bother someone else?"

Jody realized that it was pointless trying to talk to them. She turned around and waded back to shore as fast as she could. She had to tell someone. She had to stop this — before something terrible happened!

7

"Jody, what on earth has happened?" exclaimed Harry when Jody rushed aboard. "Are you all right?"

"Harry, they're feeding the dolphins!" Jody cried. Her chest hurt from running up the beach, and she'd stumbled and banged her elbow on one of the seafront lampposts. Craig and the twins had moved to another arcade, and she hadn't been able to see Gina or Brittany through the sea of shoppers, so she had run straight back to *Dolphin Dreamer.*

Harry looked confused. "Who's feeding the dolphins?"

"Tourists." Jody leaned against the mast, catching her

breath. "They were feeding them french fries, and oh, Harry! I saw Dawn the humpbacked dolphin again. They were feeding her, too!"

Dr. Taylor poked his head out of the cabin. "What's all the racket?" he asked.

Jody related her story again.

Dr. Taylor heaved a deep and knowing sigh. "What did I tell you?" he said, shaking his head. "This is a terrible place. The sooner we get out of here, the better."

"No, Dr. Taylor!" cried Jody. "Leaving's the last thing we should do! We have to help the dolphins. We have to tell someone."

Harry scratched his head. "Did you see any wardens?" he asked at last. "They'd be the ones to tell, I suppose."

Jody shook her head. "I don't think that there are any at Golden Sands," she said. "That's half the problem."

Harry looked along the pontoon at the sound of approaching feet. "Here comes your mom," he said, pointing. "She'll know what to do." He patted Jody kindly on the shoulder and disappeared to the stern of the ship.

Jody had never been so glad to see anyone in her life as Gina and Brittany made their way toward her.

"Mom, come quickly!" she called. "I have to talk to you!"

"Hi to you, too, Jody," said Brittany, sounding a bit put out.

"Sorry, Brittany, but this is an emergency," Jody apologized.

Dr. Taylor raised his hands. "I've heard the story already and offered my opinion," he said gravely. "Now I shall leave the solution to the experts."

Jody recounted what she'd seen as fast and as clearly as she could. By the time she'd finished, Gina's face was pale with shock.

"Feeding dolphins *french fries*?" she repeated, as if she could hardly believe her ears.

"Gross," Brittany said, flipping her new lilac-colored sunglasses up onto her hair.

"The dolphins will be OK, won't they?" Jody asked anxiously.

Gina sighed and shook her head. "You know the dangers of feeding wild dolphins, Jody. Anything could happen. Apart from an increasing dependency on food handouts from tourists, the dolphins are open to all kinds of problems. Poisoning, the spread of contagious diseases, obesity — they are all very real dangers. Where on earth were the wardens?"

"It's not a marine reserve like Oceans Point," Jody pointed out unhappily. "I don't think they have wardens. I didn't see any. I didn't even see any lifeguards."

Gina shook her head. "You don't have to be a marine reserve to take responsibility for your environment. There's no excuse for allowing this. The Pacific is home to so many wild creatures — it's a crime to allow them to be exploited in this way."

Jody's eyes filled with tears. "What are we going to do?"

"What's up?" Craig appeared on the deck with the twins, who promptly raced down the cabin steps to play with their new pack of Golden Sands playing cards.

Jody was halfway through the story for the fourth time when there was a loud splash off the bow.

"What was that?" Gina asked in surprise.

Jody rushed to the edge of the boat, her fears suddenly forgotten. She had the strangest feeling in her stomach. Could it be . . . ?

"Mom, Dad, come quick!" she called. She didn't care how odd she sounded. "I think it's Dawn!"

"You can't possibly know that," scoffed Brittany. "You only heard a splash!"

Jody couldn't explain the strange feeling that had come over her. "Trust me. I looked into Dawn's eyes earlier. She's come to find me."

"Dawn, the humpbacked dolphin you saw yesterday?" said Craig in astonishment. "Here?"

"I didn't get to that part, Dad," said Jody, leaning over the railing and looking up and down the harbor. "Dawn was here. She obviously swam down the coast, like Brice thought. The tourists were feeding her, too."

A fin rose and fell in the water at the mouth of the harbor. Suddenly, the surface of the water broke, and a dolphin arced up into the air.

"What unusual coloring," remarked Gina, shading her eyes. "And I can see the hump!"

At last, Jody's parents had seen her mystery dolphin.

"I knew it!" Jody said, delighted that Dawn had come to find her. "Look, she's leaping again!"

Jody watched happily as Dawn flung herself out of the water. She'd almost forgotten about the incident at the beach, this was such a beautiful sight.

"She's not leaping very high," observed Craig, frowning.

Jody thought about it. Her father was right. When she had first seen Dawn at Oceans Point, the dolphin had made a much higher leap out of the water. Now

Breaking the waves

her tail was barely leaving the surface of the water before she fell back down again.

The feeling of unease Jody had felt on the beach came surging back. Suddenly, she felt sick.

Dawn swam in circles at the mouth of the harbor, expelling air hard and fast from her blowhole.

"It looks like she's having breathing difficulties," said Gina, leaning over the boat for a better look.

"Brice said that she was looking a little overweight," said Craig. "That's probably having an effect."

With one lazy flick of her tail, Dawn disappeared beneath the water. Jody watched as the dolphin left a rippling wake behind her and swam out to sea.

"Something's wrong with her," Jody said slowly.

"I'm sure she's fine," said Brittany.

Suddenly, Jody felt as if she were calling to the tourists again and being ignored. She swung around to Brittany. "Something's wrong with that dolphin!" she shouted. "Why don't you care? Golden Sands is dirty and dangerous. I wish we'd never come!" she added passionately.

"Well, now," said a strange voice. "*Never* is a pretty strong word."

Startled, Jody looked across the water to the neighboring boat. The owner of the voice was sitting on the deck of a gleaming white pleasure cruiser, staring at her with interest.

"I said, *never* is a pretty strong word," he repeated, picking up a glass from a small table and standing up. He gestured at Jody with his drink. "What's got you so worked up, young lady?" he asked. "It's a beautiful day, and we're in a beautiful place. Golden Sands has nothing but happy vibes."

"Happy vibes?" Jody repeated. "What do you mean?"

The stranger laughed. "Just look around you! This place is all about pleasure and relaxation. The tourists are happy, the money rolls in. That's what life's about, in my book."

"Mine, too," said Brittany, staring with interest at the stranger's boat.

Jody noticed the boat's name, *Big Boy,* printed in bold red letters across the bow. Then she looked up at the seafront. All she could see were crowds and dirt, and the painful memory of Dawn taking fries from an ignorant tourist. She felt her temper rising. "People were feeding dolphins out there," she said. "They shouldn't do that."

"Hey, cool down," said the stranger, taking a long gulp from his drink. "I love dolphins. They're beautiful creatures. But they can't always find food in the ocean, so they make the best of what they can find. It's all a question of survival."

"My wife and I are marine biologists," said Craig, "and I can tell you this for a fact, sir. If dolphins become too dependent on handouts, not only do the dolphins themselves suffer, but a delicate ecological balance is lost. The cost is too terrible to consider."

The stranger shook his head, with a smile playing around his lips. "I suggest you quit worrying so much. You're on vacation, I take it? So enjoy!"

With another languid wave of his hand, he sauntered inside the cabin of *Big Boy.*

"He doesn't seem to care!" Jody said, watching him

disappear from sight. The idea that someone might not be interested in the fate of a group of wild dolphins filled her with horror.

Gina shook her head. "It seems not," she said in a resigned voice. "Come on. I think we've all had enough of Golden Sands, don't you? I suggest we get back to Oceans Point right away and report everything we've seen to Brice. If this place doesn't have wardens, you can bet your life that Brice will want to do something about it."

Jody stayed up on deck as *Dolphin Dreamer* left Golden Sands and headed for the open sea again. She needed to feel the cool, salty air on her skin, to wash away the dirt and the memories of Golden Sands. Her mind kept returning to the man on board *Big Boy*. She couldn't understand why he had been like that — so uninterested in the dolphins. He had a boat, so he obviously knew how to sail. Didn't the sea and all its natural wonders interest him at *all*?

"What do you think of my sunglasses, Jody?" Brittany appeared beside her, striking a model pose with her glasses balanced on the end of her nose. "Cool, aren't they? And they were only eight dollars."

"They're nice," said Jody absently.

"Nice?" Brittany echoed. "Is that the best you can do?"

Jody sighed. "Sorry. I'm just thinking about something else."

"No prizes for guessing what," said Brittany. "Don't worry about the dolphins," she said unexpectedly. "Brice will know what to do. He'll be able to help them."

Brittany was full of surprises, Jody thought. One minute she was a prima donna, and the next she came out with something unexpected. Maybe the McGraths' love of dolphins was rubbing off on her after all.

Dolphin Dreamer rounded the headland again, and Jody watched Oceans Point come into view. In a funny way, it felt like coming home. It was strange how attached she had become to the place, even though they'd only been there for a couple of days.

Brice was talking to the harbormaster when they arrived. Maddie, Cam, and Mei Lin were sitting in a row on the pontoon and dangling their legs in the water.

"Have a good time?" Cam called, jumping to his feet to catch the rope Harry threw at him.

"Not exactly," said Craig. "Brice, we need a word with you. Have you got a moment?"

Brice checked his watch. "Sure," he said easily. "Come on down to *Kookaburra* while I clean up. We can talk there."

"Can I come, Dad?" Jody asked.

"Of course," said Craig. "After all, you witnessed the problem. Come on."

"So, what's this about?" Brice asked as Jody and her parents both walked beside him along the battered old boardwalk toward the *Kookaburra*.

"We've just been to Golden Sands," said Jody.

Brice nodded slowly. "I think I can guess what you are about to say."

"You can?" Jody was surprised.

"We know about the resorts south of here," said Brice, jumping neatly aboard the *Kookaburra* and offering the others a hand. "Dirty and overcrowded, right?"

"More than that," said Gina grimly.

Brice was silent as Jody told him what she'd seen.

"Well," he said at last. "I knew it was bad, but not that bad. You actually saw people feeding dolphins?"

"They were feeding a dolphin french fries!" said Jody. She still found it hard to believe. "And it wasn't just any dolphin, Brice. It was Dawn. Remember you said that she was looking overweight? You were right about her scavenging around other resorts."

"We saw her in the harbor," added Craig. "She seemed to be having breathing difficulties."

Brice nodded. "That would probably be because of the extra weight," he said. "Listen, I know the owner of Golden Sands. His name is Bob Andrews. He's not a bad guy, just the kind of guy who enjoys the easy life. He probably doesn't know the half of what goes on. Why don't we pay him a visit tomorrow morning? Golden Sands is only forty minutes by car. It may be worth talking to him now that Jody has seen the situation with her own eyes. And since you guys are respected marine biologists, you'll have plenty of facts about the dangers of dolphin dependency and unregulated human contact. What do you say?"

"Let's do it," said Craig immediately. "This needs to be cleared up before any more damage is done. And when I meet Mr. Andrews, I'm going to give him a piece of my mind!"

8

March 16 — evening — on the beach at Oceans Point
Dad is swimming with Sean and Jimmy in the sunset as
I'm writing this. I know I've said that Oceans Point is
beautiful, but after Golden Sands, it's somehow magical
as well. All I can hear is the splashing of the waves (and
of Dad and the boys!) and the noisy flapping of birds'
wings as they all come home to roost in the trees behind
me. But even though it's magical, I'm restless. I want to go
to Golden Sands NOW and talk to Mr. Andrews about the
dolphins. I probably won't get any sleep tonight — I'll be

too busy worrying about Dawn. Is she OK? I wish it was
morning already. . . .

"Time to go, Jody."

Jody groaned and opened her eyes. Her mother was smiling at her.

"It's eight-thirty. Brice thought it would take about an hour to get to Golden Sands, and we want to go before the heat of the day kicks in."

Jody quickly wriggled into a T-shirt and a pair of shorts, brushed her teeth, and ran a brush through her dark hair. She walked into the kitchen, grabbed a roll and some honey, and came out on deck.

The morning was bright and cool, but the haze on the horizon suggested that it would be a hot day. Brice was waiting for them beside a battered red pickup truck, dangling a set of keys.

"It's about thirty miles," he explained as they set off, rumbling over the pits and ridges of the old Oceans Point road. "But it's a great route. The views along the coast are stunning. Enjoy!"

It felt strange taking the journey to Golden Sands by

land this time. The coastline stretched behind and ahead of them, and the multicolored beaches and cliffs gleamed in the early morning light. There were huge sand dunes all along the roadside, whipped into strange sculpted shapes by the wind and the sea.

About twenty minutes along the route, Jody saw a huge bird dive down into the sea and emerge again with a large wriggling fish clutched in its powerful talons.

"Osprey," Brice explained, expertly negotiating the odd drifts of sand that had swept across the road's surface. "We have white-breasted sea eagles, too, and peregrine falcons."

The salty smell of Golden Sands blew through the open window as Brice swung into the parking lot. "Follow me," he said, beckoning them toward the harbor.

"Does Mr. Andrews live on a boat?" asked Jody.

"He certainly does," said Brice. "It's quite a pleasure cruiser. Although to be honest, he doesn't take it out to sea very often. I think he likes the sound of the waves, but he prefers the bustle of the resort." He pointed down the pontoon to a boat moored near the mouth of the harbor. "That's his boat there."

Jody gasped. Brice was pointing at *Big Boy*. The owner of Golden Sands, Bob Andrews, was none other than yesterday's stranger!

"Brice —" she started to say.

But Brice was striding down the pontoon toward *Big Boy*, and it was too late to explain.

"This should be interesting," remarked Craig.

"He didn't listen to us yesterday," said Jody anxiously as they followed Brice toward *Big Boy*. "Why should he listen today?"

"We didn't introduce ourselves yesterday," Gina reminded her. "Perhaps when we've explained what we do, and we've had a chance to put the actual facts to him, he'll listen to us."

Jody hoped with all her heart that her mother was right. But deep down, she had a nasty feeling that it would make no difference if they introduced themselves or not. Mr. Andrews would never care, and that was that.

Brice and Bob Andrews were waiting for them on the deck of *Big Boy*.

"Hello again," said Bob Andrews smoothly when Brice made the introductions.

Brice looked confused. "You know one another?"

"We met yesterday," said Craig, extending his hand. Bob Andrews shook it genially. "We just didn't get as far as exchanging names."

Bob Andrews waved Jody and her family aboard. "Are we talking about dolphins again?" he asked.

"We are," said Gina. "We appreciate you meeting us, Mr. Andrews. We don't want to disturb your morning any more than we have to."

Bob Andrews offered them a seat in the luxurious, white leather interior of *Big Boy.* Jody noticed with interest that the boat had a glass floor like *Kookaburra.*

Bob Andrews saw Jody staring. "Like it?" he said. "You can see all kinds of things through there."

"I know," said Jody politely. "*Kookaburra* has one at Oceans Point."

While Bob Andrews fixed drinks for everyone, Brice explained that *Kookaburra* was the Oceans Point tour boat. "We like to take tourists out into deeper water, to the coast of Fraser Island," he said.

"Fraser Island, eh?" Bob Andrews handed out tea and

coffee in gleaming glass and chrome cups. "I've never been."

Jody was astonished. He had a boat, and he'd never been to Fraser Island? What did Mr. Andrews do with his time?

"The idea of the tour boat is to view dolphins and whales away from the coast," Brice said. "That way, we hope to discourage dolphins from coming too close in to shore."

"But where's the pleasure in that?" Bob Andrews objected. "The great appeal of Golden Sands is that we keep things natural." Bob Andrews was expanding on his theme. "The ocean doesn't belong to anybody. Tourists want to see dolphins for free. They don't want to pay for boat trips."

"Mr. Andrews," said Craig, "I don't think you fully understand the consequences of encouraging unsupervised human interaction with dolphins."

Bob Andrews smiled indulgently. "I assure you, Dr. McGrath, that as the owner of Golden Sands, I have never had any problem with the dolphins. The tourists love Golden Sands just the way it is. Why else would they return year after year?" He stood up. "It's been a pleasure talking to you, but I do have to be getting on with things. Would you excuse me? I'm sorry I couldn't be much help."

It was impossible to continue the conversation without appearing rude. Jody stood up slowly and followed her parents out onto the deck.

"I'm sorry you had a wasted trip," Bob Andrews began.

"Sir!" came a breathless voice from the pontoon. "Mr. Andrews, sir!"

Jody saw a young man in a bright yellow T-shirt emblazoned with the logo GOLDEN SANDS FOR A GOLDEN TIME. He seemed agitated.

"Mr. Andrews, sir!" he said again. He looked at Jody and her parents with an apologetic smile.

Bob Andrews looked irritated. "What is it, Sean?"

"It's Steven, sir," said the young man. "My name is Steven. Sorry to interrupt."

Bob Andrews raised his eyebrows. "Well?"

"Someone's found a sick dolphin, sir," Steven said.

Jody clutched her mother's arm instinctively.

Craig stepped forward. "How sick?" he said urgently.

Steven looked surprised. He glanced over at his boss.

"This is Dr. McGrath, a visiting zoologist," said Bob Andrews.

Craig didn't bother to correct him. "What are the symptoms?" he asked, stepping down from *Big Boy* onto the pontoon.

"It's hard to tell, Dr. McGrath," said Steven. "I don't really know about dolphins. I just work at the information booth on the seafront. A tourist found it."

Bob Andrews looked more alert. "A tourist?" he repeated with a frown. "That's not good."

"It looks serious, sir," said Steven anxiously. "It might even be catching."

Bob Andrews jumped down on the pontoon. "Let's go," he said.

"If the other dolphins catch it, we may have a problem on our hands," Bob Andrews said, striding up the pontoon. "The reputation of Golden Sands will suffer."

Jody turned to her mother. "What if Dawn is the dolphin who is ill?" she said anxiously.

Bob Andrews looked faintly uncomfortable. "You

can't get too attached to dolphins, young lady," he said. "They are wild creatures, and —"

"They are indeed wild," interrupted Gina grimly. "And that is why human interaction should be discouraged."

Bob Andrews opened his mouth, then closed it again. After a pause, he said, "Where is it, Steven?"

"We've penned it into a shallow area on the north beach, sir," replied the young man. They had now reached the seafront, where crowds of tourists were beginning to assemble.

Half running, half walking, Steven led them to the north beach, the one Jody hadn't explored the previous day. Jody's head was bursting with questions and worries. *What was the matter with the dolphin? Was it really as serious as Steven thought?*

At last, they reached the penned-in shallow area. Jody was shocked at the state of it. The nets looked old and mildewed, and the enclosure wasn't nearly as big as it should have been. A couple of tourists were sitting on the sand, chatting and keeping an eye on the enclo-

Dawn's very sick

sure. Jody presumed they were the ones who had found the dolphin.

She approached more closely. The sick dolphin was lying motionless on the surface of the water, its breathing fast and shallow. Jody almost cried out loud when she saw the distinctive hump below the sick animal's dorsal fin. Her worst nightmare had come true.

Brice recognized the dolphin immediately. "It's

Dawn," he said quickly. "You were right. Something is definitely wrong."

Craig looked around. "Where is the vet?" he asked Bob Andrews.

The owner of Golden Sands was biting at the nail on his little finger. Jody watched him. He was looking increasingly uncomfortable.

Steven broke the silence. "I don't think we have one, Dr. McGrath."

"You don't have a vet?" said Craig in disbelief. He waded over to the pen and gently placed his hand on Dawn's hump while he bent to listen to her breathing. Dawn rolled slightly in the water. Craig was checking the timing of Dawn's breaths against his watch. "She's definitely breathing much too rapidly," Craig said gravely. "Something is seriously wrong."

He beckoned to Gina. "Come and listen," he said. "Her breathing is labored and there's quite a strong smell to it. That's a sure sign of a respiratory infection."

Craig and Gina conferred in quiet, serious voices for a few moments. Then Craig gave the distressed dolphin a quick examination, looking carefully at her blowhole, where Jody could see some mucus oozing out. Just then, Dawn seemed to shudder and make a sneezing sound.

"Do you know what's wrong, Dad?" Jody asked in a wobbly voice. Brice put a comforting arm around her shoulders.

"I have an idea," Craig said, then stopped. "No," he corrected with a frown. "It's not possible."

"Try us," encouraged Gina, her hand resting soothingly on Dawn's back.

Craig looked up. His face was puzzled. "This is going to sound very strange," he said, slowly shaking his head, "but the closest thing I can come up with doesn't normally relate to dolphins at all." He looked at Jody. "In fact, I'm going purely on something I remember about you, Jody."

"Me?" Jody was confused.

Craig nodded. "Do you remember when you were about eight? You got so sick that we had to take you to the hospital for observation."

Jody had a faint memory of long white corridors that

smelled of pine floor cleaner and a machine that bleeped by her bed.

"If you're thinking . . ." Gina began.

Craig held up his hand. "I know it sounds crazy," he said, "but that's exactly what I'm thinking. It looks like Dawn could have a bad case of viral pneumonia. It's treatable in humans, but I've never heard of a case involving a dolphin."

He turned to Bob Andrews and looked him squarely in the eye. "If I'm right about this, Mr. Andrews, you have a very serious situation on your hands. It looks as though this animal has contracted a disease from humans. And there is a very grave danger that she will die."

9

Jody had never seen anyone look as shocked as Bob Andrews did at that moment. His jaw fell open and his deeply tanned face turned a shade of gray.

"Die?" he repeated, as if he couldn't believe what he'd just heard. "Just because it's been in contact with a few tourists?"

Craig waded back to the beach. "We need to get this animal to a vet as quickly as we can. Brice, I suggest we take her to Oceans Point in the back of your truck."

Jody stared at her dad. She knew that whenever possible, dolphins were transported by water. It was too dangerous for them to be moved any other way, because their bodies needed the water's natural support. Their internal organs could be crushed, and their skin could dehydrate.

Brice was clearly thinking the same thing. "It's a forty-minute ride by road, and we're approaching the hottest part of the day," he warned. "We may do more harm than good if we put Dawn in the truck."

"I know." Craig looked grim. "But I don't think we have any choice. It would take at least a couple of hours to move her by boat. That's too long, given the seriousness of her condition. This animal needs immediate treatment. It's a risk we have to take."

Everyone looked at the sick dolphin, who was lying quietly in the netted enclosure. Her flanks were rising and falling rapidly as she struggled to catch her breath.

"I can stay in the back of the truck with Dawn," said Jody impulsively. "I'll sluice her with water the whole way. We can put up a shade to protect her from the sun."

"We need equipment to move Dawn into the truck," said Gina. "And we need a sling to transport her properly."

117

"I already thought of that," said Brice. "After everything you told me, I put a sling in the truck, just in case. I was hoping we wouldn't have to use it."

"We still need a winch to lift her onto the truck," said Gina anxiously.

"Perhaps I can help there."

Jody turned around. In the seriousness of the situation, she had completely forgotten about Bob Andrews.

"We have a winch that we use in the harbor, for getting boats up and into dry dock for repairs," said the owner of Golden Sands. "Would that be any use?"

Craig thought about it. "Is it mobile?" he said.

"As far as I know, yes." Bob Andrews turned to Steven and gave him some brief instructions.

As Steven ran up the beach toward the harbor, Brice started running in the same direction. "I'll get the truck," he called back over his shoulder. "I'll bring it right down onto the sand, as close as I can. Then I'll need some help constructing the sling."

Jody waded into the water and approached Dawn as slowly as she could. Making soothing, clicking sounds with her tongue, she leaned over the netting. "We'll look after you," she promised, trying to sound confident. "You'll be fine once you get to Oceans Point."

She sluiced some seawater gently over Dawn's shivering back, taking care not to splash water across the dolphin's blowhole.

She felt her mother's hand on her shoulder.

"Jody, we need some water to go in the back of the truck," said Gina. "Can you fill the buckets with Mr. Andrews? He should have several on board his boat. You'll need to sluice Dawn regularly. Brice should have some kind of canopy for the truck, so we can at least shield her from the sun."

Jody nodded, grateful that her mother was trusting her with such an important task. She reluctantly tore herself away from Dawn's side and followed Bob Andrews up the beach toward *Big Boy.*

Bob Andrews didn't say a word as they approached the harbor. Jody was glad. She wasn't sure that she would be able to have a normal conversation with him after all that had happened. She obediently took the stack of large, empty buckets he handed to her and headed back down to the beach with them.

Halfway there, she looked back briefly. Bob Andrews was standing alone on the deck of *Big Boy,* watching. He raised his hand once, then walked slowly back inside the cabin.

Jody soon forgot about him as she approached the others. Craig and Gina were busy constructing the sling, and Steven had returned with the harbormaster, who had driven the harbor winch down to the beach.

Brice looked up from the back of the truck, where he was trying to fix the cradle that would hold Dawn in her sling. "Arrange the buckets on either side of this cradle, would you, Jody?" he said. "We'll fill them with seawater in a minute."

The buckets were filled with the help of an electric pump, and at last, the winch lowered the sling into the netted enclosure.

Dawn flinched briefly but was too tired and unwell to put up any kind of fight. As Craig and Gina gently fitted the sling around her inert body, the winch took up the slack. Lifting Dawn cleanly out of the water, the Golden Sands harbormaster maneuvered the sling until it was directly over the cradle in the truck.

Dawn has to get to Oceans Point — quickly!

Brice gave the thumbs-up as the sling settled into place. Then he deftly pulled up the cream-colored roof canvas and fixed it in place, providing some welcome shade. Jody scrambled onto the truck and took up her position beside Dawn.

"Ready to go!" cried Brice.

And they were off.

March 17 — afternoon — Oceans Point
I hope I never have to do anything like that road journey

again. Dawn was as good as gold, even though it was a really bumpy ride. I think I got more water on me than on Dawn, because Brice was going really fast, and it's not a very smooth road — I've got bruises all over my arms and legs. I didn't see the coastal view or anything this time. I was just concentrating on Dawn as I sluiced her over and over again. I was really glad when the truck reached Oceans Point, because I was down to my last bucket.

Brice's boss, David, is a qualified marine vet. Brice had radioed him so he knew we were coming. Brice drove straight down onto the beach and some way along until we reached a shallow inlet where David had a bag of medicine and a winch ready and waiting. Dawn is now safely in the water, but she isn't looking very good. We're taking turns watching her, in case there's any change. Please, PLEASE let Dawn be all right. I don't know what I'll do if she dies.

Jody clutched her diary as she hovered anxiously around the inlet, where her father and David Meers, the marine vet and chief warden of Oceans Point, were tending to the sick dolphin.

"Go back to the boat," Craig told her. "You'll need some rest if you're going to be on watch this evening."

Jody made a face. "Do I have to go back? I feel so useless there."

David waded out of the water. He was a tall man with spiky black hair and a deeply tanned face. He reminded Jody of someone, but she couldn't think who. "Are you taking a watch later on, young lady?" he said to her.

Jody nodded. Of course she was. She'd offered to take the midnight watch, because she knew that Dawn would need her then. She remembered being ill, waking up in the middle of the night and not being able to get back to sleep. It was the loneliest time of all.

David smiled at her. "Well, in that case you do need some rest," he urged gently.

It was one thing to argue with her father, but quite another to argue with David. Meekly, Jody left them to it, casting worried glances over her shoulder as she walked away down the beach.

She was almost at the harbor when a face she recognized appeared beside her.

"Hey, Jody," said Jason.

That's why David had looked familiar! Jody suddenly realized that he looked just like Jason. Tall, tanned — and with that unmistakable hair, which stood up even when it was soaked with seawater.

Jason saw her expression and laughed. "I guess you've just met my dad."

"How did you know?" Jody was surprised.

Jason shrugged. "People get this expression on their face when they meet us both. It's like, 'You two *must* be related.'"

Jody grinned. "You do look just like him," she agreed. She was glad for a lighter moment to lift the tension she was feeling.

They walked the last few yards to the harbor together.

"So," Jason said hesitantly. "Do you think Brittany will speak to me now?"

Jody considered the question. "She really liked the shell," she said. "I think it's worth a try."

Jason smiled with relief. "Will you tell her that I'll be on the beach for the rest of the afternoon?"

Jody agreed and waved to him as she stepped down onto the pontoon. *Dolphin Dreamer* was rocking gently in the current, looking cozy and homelike. Jody suddenly thought of her bed with longing. She was tired, she realized. It had been a long day.

Dr. Taylor was sitting on the deck with a pair of binoculars trained on the ocean horizon. He looked around at Jody's approach.

"Ah, Jody," he said gravely. "Any news on the dolphin?"

Jody hung her head and scuffed at the sand on the pontoon. "It's the same as earlier, really. David's been with her since she arrived, but it's not looking very good."

She knew that if she talked about Dawn anymore, she would cry, so she changed the subject. "Have you seen any interesting birds, Dr. Taylor?"

"I'm watching the pelicans," Dr. Taylor explained, indicating his binoculars. "A little break every now and again is important for the soul when one is engaged in important research," he added hurriedly.

Dr. Taylor's forehead and nose were red and sunburned. It was clear that he'd been spending most of his time out in the open air at Oceans Point, rather than down in his cabin with his books.

"They are quite extraordinary creatures, with their wonderful black-and-white plumage and their dark blue feet," Dr. Taylor continued with enthusiasm. "Have you seen any since our arrival?"

Jody told him about the pelicans she'd seen at Fraser Island, as well as the diving osprey on the road to Golden Sands.

The sound of an approaching boat made her turn and look out to sea. A sleek white pleasure cruiser was making its way toward the harbor. To her complete surprise, Jody realized that it was *Big Boy.*

The boat maneuvered expertly into the Oceans Point harbor and spluttered gently to a stop. Bob Andrews stepped out onto the deck.

He raised a hand slowly. "Afternoon."

"Hey, Bob." Brice appeared beside Jody, shouldering a large bag. He was obviously on his way to the inlet, to join Craig and David. "What brings you here?"

Bob Andrews slung a mooring rope at Brice, who caught it and wrapped it securely around a post. "Thought I'd come and see if I could make myself useful," he said.

Brice considered this. "Sorry, mate," he said finally. "We've got everything pretty much covered." He turned to Jody and gave her a handful of flyers. "Would you do me a favor and post these around the harbor?"

Jody looked at the flyers in her hand. "*Canceled,*" she read. "*Due to a medical emergency, the* Kookaburra *tour has been canceled until further notice.*"

She checked her watch. It was one o'clock already. People would probably be gathering at the wardens' office.

"It can't be helped," said Brice, noticing her expression. "I know it's short notice, but no one is available to take the tour. It's a shame, because Oceans Point could always use the money."

Bob Andrews spoke up. "That sounds like something I could help with."

Brice looked surprised. "You could?"

The owner of Golden Sands jumped down from the deck of his boat. "Sure," he said. "I can read a map. I may not know much about dolphins, but I can drive a boat."

"It's more than just a boat trip, Bob," said Brice. "The tourists want to hear about the wildlife as well. Do you think you know enough to keep talking for the whole tour?"

Bob Andrews looked down. After a long pause, he spoke. "When I said I don't know much about dolphins, I meant it."

For the first time, Jody could see that he was actually ashamed.

"I know," he said wryly. "People come to Golden Sands hoping to see dolphins, but what I know about wildlife you could fit on a postage stamp." He looked up at Brice. "I guess I'm not much use after all."

He stared at his feet for another moment or two, before turning around and walking back toward *Big Boy.*

Dr. Taylor stood up and carefully dusted himself off. "Perhaps I could also lend a hand?" he suggested.

Jody made the necessary introductions, and everyone shook hands.

"So how do you think you could help us, Dr. Taylor?" asked Brice with interest.

Dr. Taylor cleared his throat modestly. "I happen to know a thing or two about the birds along this coastline. I may be able to add something to the commentary."

"A bird-watching trip isn't a bad idea," Brice said thoughtfully.

Dr. Taylor blushed with pride, and Bob Andrews looked alert.

Then Brice looked anxious. "*Kookaburra* is pretty temperamental. Would you really be comfortable driving her, Bob?"

Bob Andrews grinned. "*Big Boy* has a glass floor and can take about a dozen passengers or so. What do you say?"

Jody watched Brice's face split into a large smile. "You're on!" he exclaimed.

March 17 — evening — Dolphin Dreamer

The Big Boy *trip went really well. Dr. Taylor hasn't stopped talking about it. They actually landed at Fraser Island and took a guided walk. Bob Andrews said he'd*

always wanted to go there. They saw birds like pied oys-
tercatchers and pelicans and watched a brahminy kite
dive down for fish. And Dr. Taylor's prize sighting was a
ground parrot — apparently it's one of the rarest birds in
Australia! The high point of the trip for Bob Andrews was
spotting a dingo sunning itself on one of the rocks by
the beach, but it soon disappeared when he tried to get
closer.

Dr. Taylor had been humming a happy little tune ever
since he'd returned from the *Big Boy* tour. He'd clearly
had a fantastic time and had become good friends with
Bob Andrews. He cornered Jody that afternoon and insisted on showing her a couple of his bird books.

"Look," he said, pointing. "This is a jabiru. See its mar-
velous long red legs? Apart from its long, thin beak, I always think it resembles a black-and-white flamingo.
And this is a brolga. A remarkable bird. We saw one
nesting on one of the Fraser Island lakes. Quite aston-
ishing. And the rainbow lorikeets — I tell you, you've
never seen such colorful little birds."

Jody was trying hard to concentrate on what Dr. Taylor was telling her, but her mind kept straying to Dawn. She was on the midnight watch tonight. She checked her watch. Five hours to go.

Dr. Taylor closed his book with an apologetic smile. "I'm sorry, Jody," he said. "I do tend to get a little carried away with my birds, don't I? But I can see that you have something else on your mind."

"Those birds look amazing," Jody said honestly. "I'm really happy that you saw them, Dr. Taylor. But I can't help thinking about Dawn."

"Quite understandable," said Dr. Taylor. "Don't let me keep you any longer."

And he strode back to his cabin, whistling a little tune quietly to himself.

Jody started to climb up the steps onto the deck. She wanted to go back to the inlet, just to check . . .

"Oh, no, you don't!" Gina stood in front of Jody with her hands on her hips. "You need some sleep, Jody. I'm not having you on any midnight watch unless you get at least four hours rest beforehand. So if I were you, I'd head straight back to your cabin and get ready for bed. Is that clear?"

131

Jody slowly walked back to her cabin. Brittany wasn't there. She'd grinned with delight as soon as Jody had given her Jason's message and rushed off the boat without a second glance. Jody guessed Jason was truly forgiven now.

She undressed and brushed her teeth. Her little cabin bed did look inviting, with its cool white sheets and soft pillows. She climbed in and settled down, tucking her hands behind her head and staring up at the little skylight, which still showed a clear blue patch of sky.

There was a knock at the door, and Jody's dad walked in.

"Settling down for a few hours?"

"Something like that," said Jody.

Craig sat on the edge of Jody's bed. "Jody, you do know that Dawn's condition isn't very hopeful, don't you?" he said after a pause.

Jody nodded, trying hard to be brave.

Craig looked down at his hands. "We have to remember that we can't save every sick dolphin we find," he said. "No matter what we do, sometimes a dolphin's time is up."

Jody was silent. She knew her dad was trying to prepare her for the worst, and it left her with a sick feeling in her stomach.

"Sleep well," said Craig, kissing her and standing up. "I'll call you when it's time for your watch."

Jody stared up at the skylight again as the cabin door swung shut. Four more hours. She knew she wouldn't sleep a wink.

Somehow, the hours passed. Jody tossed and turned in the dark and drifted into anxious dreams. One dream was so vivid that she jerked awake with a pounding heart, imagining that Dawn had died in the night.

"Are you OK?" Brittany whispered across the room. "You were making a really funny noise."

Jody shook her head, trying to clear it. "Yes," she said after a moment. "I'm fine. It was just a dream."

But was it? She checked her watch. It was just after eleven-thirty. She scrambled out of bed and pulled on a sweatshirt and jeans. She knew the night air would be chilly.

"Good luck," said Brittany sleepily. "I hope Dawn's OK."

The moonlight was bright, casting strange, long shadows across the beach. Jody met her father halfway down the sandy shore.

"How is she?" Jody asked immediately.

Craig smiled wearily. "She's still with us," he said. "I don't know where she's getting the strength from. She hasn't eaten anything all day."

"She wants to survive," said Jody, suddenly certain of it.

Craig gave a tired chuckle. "You just might be right," he said. "There's no other explanation for it." He touched Jody lightly on the shoulder. "David will be back in a couple of hours. Just stay with Dawn until he comes, OK? The only thing we can do for her now is keep her company."

Jody quickly ran down to the inlet. The moon had painted the sea silver, and there was a strange hush in the air.

Dawn was lying motionless in the water. Jody held her fingers above the dolphin's blowhole and felt only the faintest breath. But she was still breathing.

Jody settled down on the sand and started to talk. She told Dawn about all the places they had visited on *Dolphin Dreamer.* She described the dolphins they had worked with and the people they had met. She told her about the different climates and the huge variety of birds and animals they had seen. She talked about her friends back home, about her school and her life in Florida. Somehow, she knew that Dawn was listening and that hearing the sound of Jody's voice was soothing her. Jody felt a special bond with the sick dolphin and promised herself fiercely that there was still hope. For as long as it took, she would keep talking.

"Talking to yourself?"

Jody jumped up when she saw David.

"Dad said you'd be at least two hours!" she said in surprise.

David checked his watch. "Well, I don't know what

time you came down here, but it's two o'clock in the morning now."

Jody couldn't believe it. How had she talked for so long? She looked at Dawn. The dolphin was as motionless as she had been at midnight, but her blowhole was still gently opening and closing. Would she pull through?

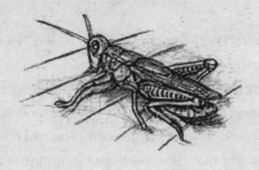

10

March 18 — morning — at the waterfront café in Oceans Point
Dawn lasted the night. I knew she would! I went to see
her first thing this morning. Brittany was already down
there with Jason, who took this morning's early watch. I
couldn't believe it when I woke up and Brittany's bed
was empty! I'm pleased that she's happy again. Now we
just have to keep our fingers crossed for Dawn.

Jody approached the inlet. It was the third time she'd
visited Dawn that day. She just couldn't stay away, in
case there was any change.

Brice and David were both in the water. They waved when they saw Jody.

"Any improvement?" she said hopefully.

There was a short silence as David and Brice exchanged glances. Jody's heart sank. She had felt so positive last night that Dawn was going to improve.

"She's not getting any better, is she?" she said, biting her lip to keep it steady.

David shook his head gently. He looked tired. "Her health was poor to start with," he said. "For a dolphin to battle something like this, it would have needed to be strong and well initially. To make things worse, this is a particularly nasty human form of pneumonia, as your dad suspected. We're running out of time, Jody."

Jody looked at Dawn, who was lying ominously still in the enclosed inlet. Her eyes were half closed. Even her hump seemed smaller, and her dorsal fin was flopping sadly off to one side.

David spoke again. "It's unkind to prolong her suffering. Unless she responds within the next two hours, I'm afraid we will have to discontinue the treatment."

"No!" Jody cried defiantly. "We won't! We can't!" she cried as David's words sank in.

"It's not fair to Dawn, Jody," said Brice, putting his arm around her shoulders. "You know how cruel it is to let an animal suffer when there's no hope."

Jody turned to him, her expression fierce. "There *is* hope!" she insisted. "We can't give up. I know Dawn can get through this!"

She turned and fled up the beach, tears blurring her eyes. She ran as fast as she could, not caring where she was going.

"Hey!"

She felt two strong arms catch her around the waist and lift her off the sand. It was her dad.

Jody burst into tears. Craig just held her and stroked her head. Jimmy and Sean stopped their games and came over to stand quietly beside their sister. They seemed to know that this wasn't the time for jokes or tricks.

At last, through hiccups and sniffles, Jody managed to tell her dad what David had said.

"Well!" Craig exclaimed. "What are you worrying for? He said we still had a couple of hours to hope, didn't he? Look on the bright side, Jody!"

Jody quietened down and concentrated on breathing steadily and calmly. "Two hours isn't long," she said.

"But it might just be long enough," replied Craig.

Jody looked at her dad's crinkled blue eyes and felt her spirits lifting a little.

Craig pointed to a picnic blanket under the trees. Mei Lin had laid out a feast of food — cold tuna, a brightly colored bean salad, mounds of floury white rolls, and wedges of cheese. Gina and Maddie were unpacking a cooler filled with bottles of lemonade. Cameron was wrestling with a coconut, which he was trying to pierce with his penknife. Jody could see that the food looked fantastic, but her stomach was rebelling. She just wasn't hungry, not with Dawn so ill.

"It's lunchtime," Craig said encouragingly. "Let's go have something to eat. You'll be more use to Dawn with some food inside you, OK?"

Jody dutifully put a few bits and pieces of food on her plate. She hadn't had any breakfast because of her

Looks like fun!

early start, and it was already past twelve o'clock. But the soft white rolls tasted like cotton and the tuna like cardboard. She ate mechanically and thought about Dawn the whole time.

At last, her plate was empty. Jody looked up dully and realized that Brittany was nowhere to be seen.

"Where's Brittany?" she said at last.

"Out with her *boyfriend,*" sang Jimmy mockingly.

Sean dissolved into giggles.

141

"She's gone snorkeling with Jason," said Gina, passing Jody a piece of creamy white coconut. "Those two really seem to have hit it off. I must say, I almost miss the cranky Brittany we all know and love."

When lunch was over, Jody felt strangely sleepy. Lulled by the swishing of the wind through the trees above her, she drifted off into an odd, dream-filled sleep. Images of pelicans, dugongs, ospreys, and dolphins floated through a watery world in her mind. All the dolphins looked like Dawn.

She awoke with a start. Dawn! What time was it? How long had she been asleep?

She could see her parents at the water's edge with her brothers. Maddie and Cameron were sitting together under a tree a little farther along the beach, chatting quietly. She checked her watch. It was one-thirty — more than an hour and a half since she had left Dawn with David and Brice.

Jumping to her feet, she looked toward the inlet. She was too far away to see anything, so she started to run. She ran down the beach as fast as she could. It seemed much farther away than she remembered.

At last, she reached it. But she couldn't ask the question. She just stared at David, who was wading out of the water toward her.

"It's OK," said David. "She's responding." His face broke into a huge grin. "This is one tough animal, Jody. She's going to pull through."

March 19 — morning — sitting on the sand at the inlet
I cried all over again when David told me that Dawn was going to be OK. Dawn's eyes were open, and she even clicked at me, though she was pretty weak. Somehow she found the strength to keep fighting. David could hardly believe it. By evening, she was starting to get restless, banging her tail from side to side and tossing her head. David wanted to keep her under observation for one more night, just in case. I found them feeding her some fish this morning. She couldn't get enough of it. Maybe french fries from a greasy paper bag won't taste so nice in the future!

Jody tucked away her diary and took a handful of warm sand, letting it run slowly through her fingers.

They had all gathered at the inlet to watch Dawn being released back into the ocean. Brittany was there with Jason. Jimmy and Sean had built a sand castle and were standing on top of it, fighting for the best view. Craig and Gina were chatting with David and Brice, and Mei Lin, Harry, Dr. Taylor, Cam, and Maddie were all watching from a distance.

David turned to Jody. "Would you do the honors?" he asked.

Jody got to her feet, her stomach tightening in anticipation. She looked at the netting that sectioned off the inlet from the rest of the sea. Carefully, she unhooked the net and rolled it slowly across to the other side. The way to the deep blue sea was now open. Would Dawn take it?

With a powerful beat of her tail, Dawn shot through the opening. Within moments, all they could see of her was a powerful wake, streaming after her like a long silken ribbon. Then that, too, disappeared.

Jody felt disappointed. Was that it?

Gina came to stand beside her. "It's a good sign, Jody," she said encouragingly. "It means that Dawn felt well enough to turn her back on us and return to the sea without a second glance."

Jody walked slowly back up the beach toward *Dolphin Dreamer* with the others. Mei Lin had arranged a big celebratory lunch, and everyone was invited.

Bob Andrews was waiting for them in the harbor. He'd brought *Big Boy* back to Oceans Point that morning, and he was full of plans that he couldn't wait to share.

"I've decided to use *Big Boy* to run tours at Golden Sands," he announced. "What do you think?"

"That's great!" Craig gave a genuine smile. "Good luck to you."

Bob Andrews waved his hand. "I still maintain that I can only drive a boat," he said. "But Steven — remember him? It turns out that he's eager to learn more about dolphins since he found Dawn the other day. He's already learned a whole lot of impressive stuff, so I thought I'd employ him on the boat as my commentator." Then he looked across at Dr. Taylor. "And this clever guy has provided me with some terrific notes on the birds we saw at Fraser Island. So we can run bird-watching tours on the island as well."

145

Dr. Taylor looked so pleased that Jody thought he might burst into tears. "I'm honored to have been able to h-help," he stuttered.

Bob Andrews suddenly looked serious. "But my most important decision is to start employing wardens," he said. "It's time that we had some kind of system in place to stop the feeding. I never want to go through that business again, and I'm pretty sure the dolphins don't, either."

"We'll drink to that," declared Gina, raising her glass.

"A toast, then!" said Craig, rapping the side of *Dolphin Dreamer* to catch everyone's attention. "To a new enterprise and happy dolphins."

"To a new enterprise and happy dolphins!" everyone chorused.

And with a clink of glasses, the party went into full swing.

March 19 — siesta time — aboard Dolphin Dreamer
Everyone's sleeping off their lunch now. Bob Andrews has gone back to Golden Sands, and the food has been cleared away. It was a fantastic party. So why don't I feel

happier? I know it's selfish of me, but I really thought Dawn would have said good-bye. I sensed a connection with her, but I guess I was wrong.

"Jody?" Sean tugged at his sister's sleeve.

"What is it?" Jody asked, putting her diary carefully down on the deck.

"There's a bug on the deck," he said. "We don't know what it is, and it's really huge!"

"Where . . . ?" Jody started to say. Then she remembered.

"Oh, no," she said, shaking her head and picking up her diary again. "You're not going to get me a second time, OK? That's a really old joke now, Sean."

"No, really!" Sean protested.

Jimmy came running up. "Jody, you've got to come!" he said. "Everyone else is asleep!"

Jody looked around. Her parents were down in their cabin, Dr. Taylor was snoozing in his deck chair, and Brittany and Jason appeared to be fast asleep on the cabin roof, side by side on Brittany's towel.

Jody sighed. "Jimmy, forget it! It was funny the first time around, but not now."

A sudden movement caught her eye. She looked around to see the most enormous insect leap across the deck. Jimmy and Sean shrieked.

"It's a grasshopper!" Jody gasped.

The grasshopper was bright green and looked almost exactly like a leaf. Jimmy and Sean were right. It was enormous.

It paused in the middle of the deck. Then in one flying leap, it took off and landed smack in the middle of Dr. Taylor's lap.

Dr. Taylor woke abruptly from his snooze. He let out a great bellow of fright and jumped to his feet as if his shorts were on fire. "Get it off me!" he roared.

And he leaped over the side of the boat and into the water with an enormous splash.

After a shocked silence, Jimmy and Sean collapsed into howls of laughter. Jody hurried to the side of the boat and peered into the water. "Are you OK, Dr. Taylor?" she asked anxiously.

Choking and spluttering, Dr. Taylor surfaced. His face was bright red and his eyes were bulging. He'd clearly had the most terrible shock.

"Unreal!" cried Brittany from the cabin roof.

Dr. Taylor bobbed around in the water, opening and shutting his mouth like a fish. At last, he managed to speak. "What was that?"

Jody was about to break the news to him that it was only a harmless grasshopper, when another splash just outside the harbor drew her attention.

A long, thin, pink-and-white-splashed beak rose from the water. It was followed by a domed pinkish head and an unmistakable hump.

Dawn floated on the surface of the water, expelling air gently from her blowhole. Then she rolled back under the water again.

Jody held her breath and watched. Suddenly, the dolphin flew up into the air in a graceful arc, flipping her tail once before plunging back into the water. She had come to say good-bye after all.

Dolphin Diaries™

Look for Dolphin Diaries #10

Beyond the Sunrise

Shiv peered over the side of the boat. "Have you seen any dolphins yet?" he asked.

Almost in answer to his question, the water broke about fifty yards ahead of the boat, and the sleek, gray body of a dolphin could be seen.

"Mom, Dad!" called Jody in excitement. "The dolphins are here!"

She watched closely as the water broke again. Was it an Irrawaddy? Could it be the same one she and Shiv had seen the previous day, before they had met Mr. Vikram?

"It's a Susu," said Craig from behind her.

"Susie?" said Jody, confused. Since when did this dolphin have a name?

"No, not Susie!" Gina laughed, putting her arm around Jody's shoulders. "Susu. It's another name for a Ganges river dolphin. This one is female, I think."

"Then I think we should call her Susie," said Jody promptly.

Susie the dolphin breached again. This time Jody could see a long, toothed beak poking above the water.

"Why does she hold her beak above the water like that?" she asked in fascination.

"Just sociable, I think." Craig laughed.

Susie began a series of very fast clicks and whistles, nodding her strange, long beak in the air.

"She's definitely sociable," said Jody. "She's trying to talk to us!"

She leaned over the railing to get a closer look. Susie immediately spun over on one side, and waved a flipper at Jody, who laughed with delight.

"I think she's feeding," said Gina. "They use their flippers to sift through the mud on the riverbed, looking for food."

With one final, cheerful whistle, Susie slipped below the churning surface of the river and was gone.

"I'm glad you've seen a dolphin at last," said Harry, stepping over to join them at the rail. Ravi and Sunnu followed him, talking quietly together. "I've seen a few from the *Dolphin Dreamer* these past couple of nights."

"What else have you seen, Harry?" Jody asked.

"Crocodiles," said Harry promptly. "They're tough looking. But you know that big one from the other day? Apparently, the fishermen haven't seen her since that morning. Maybe she's found some other fishermen to steal from."

Shiv looked surprised. "I have never known Chalaka to miss a catch," he said.

Ravi and Sunnu also looked surprised, Jody thought. No, more than that — they looked *concerned*.

"When did the fishermen last see her?" Ravi asked.

"Like I told you," said Harry. "Yesterday morning, at the catch."

Ravi and Sunnu exchanged a strange, silent glance. Jody was about to ask them what they were thinking, but her attention was distracted by two or three brightly

153

colored birds — kingfishers, according to Dr. Taylor — which flew like lightning across the river. And then she forgot all about it.

The sun was already quite high in the sky when *Dolphin Dreamer* reached Mongla. It felt like a different country from the peace and quiet of the Sukhi Rest House. Hundreds of people were milling along the riverbank, browsing at the market stalls that had been set up along the water. Boats of all shapes and sizes had docked at the long bamboo jetty, and Jody could hear lively music floating across the water.

"Mongla likes to enjoy itself on market day," Shiv said to her as they all made their way up the jetty and into the town. "Making music and making money — they go together very well, don't you think?"

Harry checked his watch. "Cam and I will make our way to the boatyard," he said. "Ravi, can you show us where to go?"

"Then I suggest we all meet back at the boat in two hours," said Craig, looking at the rest of them.

Mei Lin's eyes gleamed. "I'll enjoy putting together a

banquet fit for a king with groceries from these." She laughed, indicating the market stalls. "Brittany, can you help me? We will find some wonderful food, I am sure."

"I don't envy the traders," remarked Gina as Mei Lin and Brittany headed into the heart of the market. "I think Mei Lin will drive a hard bargain!"

Everyone went their separate way, promising to meet back at the boat at midday.

"Come on," said Shiv, grabbing Jody's hand and pulling her into the market. "Two hours isn't long for Mongla!"

Jody felt overwhelmed by the color and energy of the town as Shiv dragged her from place to place. There were piles of exotic fruit, bales of brightly colored cotton and silk, squawking chickens, and bleating goats everywhere. The air was warm and full of the smells of Sundarban life — animal and vegetable, burning incense, and muddy river water. Jody peered into stalls where men were having their hair cut, eating bowls of steamed fish, even having their teeth looked at by a market dentist. She saw stalls covered with wicker cages of tiny singing birds, who filled the air with trilling and chattering. And she heard cheerful music pumping from every stall and every house along the way.

"Let's go and find Harry," said Shiv at last. "We must be back at the boat in a little while. Maybe he needs some help."

They wandered down a side alley to the river, where they found a large open-sided building on the waterfront. Boats in various stages of repair lay in front of it on the riverbank, and the inside of the building was filled with sounds of hammering and banging.

Jody peered around, trying to catch sight of Harry. Two men were talking at the far end of the boatyard. One of the men looked familiar — but it wasn't Harry.

"It's Mr. Vikram!" said Jody in surprise.

Shiv hissed through his teeth. "He will probably shout at us again if he sees us," he said. "I think we should stay back here for now."

They crouched down and watched from a safe distance.

"He is talking to Khaled, the owner," Shiv explained, frowning. "But it is a very strange conversation."

"Mr. Vikram must be getting his boat fixed," said Jody.

Shiv shook his head. "I think he is ordering a new boat. But maybe I heard wrong. Mr. Vikram has no money — his shellfish business is not doing so well at the moment, I know."

They listened some more. Mr. Vikram was waving his hands, and so was Khaled.

Shiv straightened up. "I think we should go back to *Dolphin Dreamer*," he said. "Maybe my parents will understand this better than I do. Because Mr. Vikram was definitely buying a boat. And I don't know how that is possible."